"I don't remember asking you to wash my back."

"Of course you did," Sam replied. "You ask me to touch you every time you look at me, whenever you smile at me with those soft, inviting lips. Your skin flames when I touch you. Here. And here."

His fingers traced a line of fire down her throat and around each breast, leaving sparks on her skin. Davina was burning for him, her need unrestrained. She pulled his head down to her lips. "Kiss me," she demanded. "Really kiss me."

His thumbs brushed against her nipples as he gave her a long, deep kiss. She tasted delicious. Sweet. Forbidden. "You're incredible," he said huskily. "Where have you been all my life?"

"Boston," she whispered. "I've been in Boston."

The flames that had been flickering between them flared, and he murmured, "At last I've found something to love about Boston."

JoAnn Ross is a wonderfully prolific writer with such a vivid imagination that she never fails to delight us and readers with each new story. She was drawn to the setting for *Hot on the Trail* by her interest in Mayan culture, and to the theme by her love of vicarious adventure. "Real adventure," she says with characteristic humor, "is hard to come by when you're alone with your word processor."

JoAnn and her husband live in Phoenix, Arizona.

Books by JoAnn Ross

HARLEQUIN TEMPTATION

77–DUSKFIRE
96–WITHOUT PRECEDENT
115–A HERO AT HEART
126–MAGIC IN THE NIGHT
137–PLAYING FOR KEEPS
153–TEMPTING FATE

HARLEQUIN INTRIGUE

27–RISKY PLEASURE
36–BAIT AND SWITCH

Don't miss any of our special offers. Write to us at the following address for information on our newest releases.

Harlequin Reader Service
901 Fuhrmann Blvd., P.O. Box 1397, Buffalo, NY 14240
Canadian address: P.O. Box 603,
Fort Erie, Ont. L2A 5X3

Hot on the Trail

JoANN ROSS

Harlequin Books

TORONTO • NEW YORK • LONDON
AMSTERDAM • PARIS • SYDNEY • HAMBURG
STOCKHOLM • ATHENS • TOKYO • MILAN

For Cherry Campbell Wilkinson,
who can always make me laugh,
even when it hurts

Published September 1987

ISBN 0-373-25271-4

1

DAVINA LOWELL was an attractive woman. A damned good-looking woman, Sam McGee amended. She was also trouble with a capital *T*—trouble he had every intention of avoiding. He sat in the shadows nursing his drink as he watched her struggle to adjust to the lighting—no small feat, considering the contrast between the blazing outdoor sun and the dimly lit cantina. Eventually successful, she began tentatively looking around the room.

While her dark blond hair and light-colored eyes—either blue or green; at this distance he couldn't quite tell—gave evidence that she was not a local, her impatient air indicated she could have come from another planet. If she was going to hang around Calderitas, she was going to have to learn to relax, Sam considered idly.

Then he shook his head in self-disgust. His mind must be going soft from the tequila he'd drunk today. That woman stick around here? He eyed the bottle suspiciously; next thing he knew, he'd be tidying up the place for Princess Di.

It was the weather, Sam assured himself, seeking an excuse for his uncharacteristic drinking. The temperature was in the nineties, the humidity nearly as high. The predawn thunderstorm, instead of cooling things down, had only added to the stultifying discomfort. The still air was pregnant with moisture, rendering the rusty paddle-blade fan next to useless as it creaked slowly and steadily overhead.

The monsoons had driven more than one man to drink. When the rainy season came to this lonely, barren Yucatán

Peninsula, the crime rate rose, doctors reported an increase in headaches, neuralgia and nervous complaints, and the hospitals' psychiatric wards became more crowded with each passing day.

Still, Sam was forced to admit, he had never been one of those adversely affected by the monsoons. He had taken them in stride, as he took the heat, the dust, the blazing Mexican sun—and the isolation.

When that excuse fell depressingly flat, he tried telling himself that today's birthday was to blame; after all, forty was a milestone in a man's life—a time to take stock of the past, to weigh deeds and misdeeds as one would entries in a ledger. Since that idea hit a little too close to home, he wondered how many years would have to go by before he could forget the past and look forward to the future. He had exiled himself from friends and family for five long, desolate years, and the pain had not ceased.

It had admittedly lessened somewhat. At least now he was able to forget that debacle in the Amazon for days, sometimes weeks, at a time. That in itself could probably be seen as progress, Sam decided; down here one measured such things with a different yardstick than in the civilized world.

Uncomfortable with such introspection, Sam returned his attention to Davina Lowell. He'd never seen a woman so obviously out of her realm. Unaware of Sam McGee's silent study, Davina surveyed the patrons of the tavern with definite misgivings. Although she hadn't expected Cary Grant, she had been hoping for someone who at least didn't remind her of an escapee from a chain gang. Any one of half a dozen men could be the individual she had come here to meet; not one of them looked at all promising. Taking a deep breath, Davina reminded herself of the importance of her mission as she crossed the room to the bar, her head held high, her spine stiff.

The bartender proved to be the most promising subject yet but, in his mid-twenties, he was too young. His dark-brown eyes surveyed her with overt appreciation.

"*Señorita*," he greeted her, his smile a flash of white in a dark complexion. "What can I do for you?"

"I'm looking for a man," Davina began tentatively, aware of the fact that she had garnered the attention of every male in the room. She could feel several pairs of dark eyes burning holes in her back.

With fingers that trembled only slightly, she dug into the pocket of her slim cotton skirt. She didn't need to turn around to know that the cantina's clientele found the gesture fascinating. Despite her nervousness, Davina managed to extract a folded piece of paper, which she handed to the bartender.

"This man," she said.

The young man's eyes widened as he read the name. "Are you sure this is the man you seek?"

Davina inclined her head. "Very sure," she answered with far more aplomb than she was feeling at the moment. "I was told that I could find him here."

For some reason that Davina could not discern, the bartender appeared caught between dueling loyalties. She was familiar enough with the Latin male to know that above all, he relished the opportunity to be of any small service to a lady. Yet something was definitely keeping this man from revealing the whereabouts of her quarry.

Watching the little drama from his table concealed in the shadows, Sam shook his head in disgust. While her plain cotton blouse and skirt were a far cry from a seductive ensemble, they couldn't entirely conceal her slender but decidedly feminine curves. Didn't she realize that for a lone woman to walk into a place like this was like waving a red cape in front of a bull? Heaving a weary sigh of resignation, he pushed himself up from the table.

"Is there a problem?"

At the sound of an obviously American accent, Davina spun around, looking upward into a pair of tawny-gold eyes. "No problem at all," she said. "I was merely asking the bartender a question."

"Is that so?" Sam's slow, lazy gaze moved over her. Her eyes, he noted, were neither blue nor green, but an incredible shade of turquoise. "Perhaps I might know the answer."

Davina didn't like the masculine glint in the man's eyes. She belatedly realized that by coming in here without an escort, she had put herself in a perilous position. But it wasn't as if she had been given any choice. Besides, if she couldn't handle one expatriate American masher, she had no business being here in the first place.

"I doubt it." Her clipped tones designed to dismiss the rude stranger, Davina turned her attention back to the bartender. "Do you know where I can find Mr. McGee?"

"Why are you looking for McGee?" the deep voice behind her asked.

Davina didn't bother to restrain her irritation at the interruption. She was hot, tired, sweaty and losing patience by the minute. She hadn't come all the way to the Yucatán Peninsula of Mexico to play Twenty Questions.

"That's between Mr. McGee and myself," she snapped.

Sam took her arm, deliberately turning her away from the bar. "Then you're in luck, sweetheart," he drawled. "Because you've just found him."

As she stared up at the man, Davina's bleak gaze took in the hard amber eyes, the grim smile framed by several days' growth of black stubble. On top of his less-than-admirable appearance, she could detect the unmistakable aroma of alcohol.

"Don't tell me that *you're* Sam McGee?" she asked with a groan.

"Don't worry that pretty little head about a thing." Sam assured her. "While I'll admit that you're not seeing me at my best, I assure you that I'm up to anything you have to offer." His grin, rakishly suggestive, held no genuine warmth.

"I came here to discuss business," Davina insisted, digging in her heels as he appeared prepared to drag her across the floor.

If he was at all disturbed by her stiff tone, Sam gave no evidence of it. "So come into my office and we'll talk," he said, leading her to the table at the back of the room. "Luis," he called out to the bartender, "get the lady a drink." He eyed her thoughtfully. "A margarita."

"I'd prefer water," Davina objected. "It's a great deal warmer than I expected."

"It's the humidity; not many tourists come down here during the rainy season. Actually, not many tourists make it down here to Calderitas the rest of the year, either," Sam amended. "Make that a glass of water," he shot back over his shoulder. "And a margarita."

He slung his body back into the recently vacated chair. "Something wrong?" he asked, looking up at Davina curiously when she remained standing beside the table.

Davina wondered what on earth had made her expect this roughneck to hold her chair for her. She sat down and folded her hands primly in her lap.

"Nothing's wrong," she assured him with feigned calm. As she heard the outrageous falsehood leave her lips, Davina decided it had to be the understatement of the century. From the moment her plane had landed, she had been experiencing a vague, ominous feeling of impending disaster. "If you don't mind, Mr. McGee, I'd like to get right down to business."

He held up his hand. "Whoa, right there, lady. As a matter of fact, I damn well do mind. I don't know how it is where you come from, but down here in Calderitas, we don't believe in rushing things."

"I understand that, but—"

"Unless it's friendships." He poured a splash of the clear liquid into a glass. "Are you in favor of cultivating new friendships?" he asked amiably.

"In the right circumstances. With the right people."

Sam's eyes narrowed as he sipped the drink thoughtfully. "That might tend to narrow the field a bit."

"It most certainly does," Davina agreed briskly. "Now. Mr. McGee, about my business offer—"

"Call me Sam," he invited expansively. "We don't go in for formalities down here." He threw back his head and tossed off the tequila. When he refilled the glass once again, Davina made the decision that it was past time to leave.

"Well, this has certainly been an enlightening conversation," she said brightly, not wanting to do anything to set him off. Davina had the distinct feeling that Sam McGee could be a very dangerous man if pushed. "But it appears that I was mistaken, Mr. McGee. I'm afraid I was looking for someone else."

When she made a move to rise from the table, iron fingers suddenly curled around her wrist. "Sit down."

He had not raised his voice but there was a dark, ominous look in his eyes that affected her more harshly than the loudest shout. She sank back down onto the wicker chair.

"Really, Mr. McGee, I have to be leaving if I'm going to catch the afternoon flight out of town."

"You haven't had your drink yet." He glanced over her shoulder. "Here comes Luis now. You wouldn't want him to think you didn't appreciate all his efforts to make that margarita, would you?" He gave her a mirthless smile. "Most of our patrons are willing to settle for something a helluva lot less fancy."

Realizing that at that moment she wasn't presented with a myriad of choices, Davina weakly smiled her gratitude to Luis as he placed her drinks on the scarred wooden table. The young man smiled back encouragingly. Then, taking in Sam's granite face, he backed away from the table and faded into the smoke-filled room.

Forgetting every lesson she had ever been taught about drinking foreign water, Davina gulped it down thirstily. Coming at this moment, after that long hot flight and the dusty walk to the cantina, the icy liquid tasted better than Dom Perignon.

"You do that very well," she said at length, feeling worlds better now that she had quenched her thirst.

Sam's only response was an arched brow.

Davina tilted her head in the direction of the bar. "That air of silent intimidation. Poor Luis looked as if he were afraid you'd break him in half if he so much as uttered a single word to me."

There was a rough, gravelly sound to Sam's answering laughter, as if he didn't do it very often. "'Poor Luis' killed a man with a knife before he'd celebrated his twelfth birthday. What makes you think I could intimidate someone like that?"

Davina didn't have to consider her answer for more than a fleeting second. "He may have killed someone," she said decisively, her turquoise eyes drifting back across the room to study the young man who was busily wiping the bar with a rag, pretending to ignore her silent scrutiny. "But it was

in self-defense. And even then the act didn't come easily."
Her gaze was calm as it settled on Sam's face. "You, on the
other hand, would probably have no compunction about
killing another human being."

He eyed her over the rim of his glass. "You seem to have
me all figured out."

She waved away his words with a delicate flick of her
wrist. "You're not that complex."

"Is that a fact?"

"I've dealt with thousands of men a great deal like you."

It was Sam's turn to look surprised. "Thousands?"

If she was a hooker, she was without a doubt the classi-
est one he'd ever seen. And that included those who resided
in decorated Manhattan penthouses that cost more to
maintain for a week than this place earned in a year. He
wondered if she could actually be suggesting working here.

Is that why she had spent the day going all over town
looking for him? Word of Davina Lowell's arrival had
spread like wildfire, and he was forced to admit to some curiosity as to why she was searching him out.

For some reason he could not discern, Sam was vaguely
disappointed to discover her motive was one of the oldest
in the book. Putting her to work would certainly draw the
tourist crowd, he was forced to consider for a moment.
Then, reminding himself of all the reasons he was living here
in the Yucatán, miles from civilization, he sighed.

"Sorry, sweetheart, but I'm not hiring any girls right now.
Not that you wouldn't bring some class to the joint, but I
run a clean shop. No smuggled artifacts, no drugs, no girls."

He shrugged as he took another drink of the tequila. "Not
that I wouldn't be willing to sample a bit of your hospital-
ity—just in case you need a reference."

As Sam's words sank in, Davina stared at him, not
knowing whether she should feel flattered by the fact that

he thought her attractive enough to make a living selling her body, or enraged that he'd believe her willing to ply her trade in what could only charitably be called a dump.

"You're drunk."

He lifted his glass in a silent salute. "The lady's perceptive as well as beautiful. However, in this case, you're dead wrong, sweetheart. I'm a long, long way from being drunk—unfortunately."

Davina had no intention of sitting by, watching this uncouth lout drink himself into oblivion. Besides, in ten minutes the plane would be taking off. If she didn't make it there in time, she'd have to spend the night in this unappealing waterfront town. At the moment, she couldn't think of any less attractive scenario.

"I wish you the best of luck in your endeavor," she said stiffly. "If you keep it up, you should be out cold in no time at all. Now, if you'd be so kind as to unhand me, I'd like to leave."

Sam glanced down at Davina's slender wrist, as if he had forgotten he was still holding it. "Can't," he finally said. "You haven't sampled Luis's margarita yet."

Davina tugged her arm, discovering that she had only succeeded in encouraging his fingers to tighten further. "I don't suppose it would do any good to threaten to scream?"

He shook his head. "Nope. People around here tend not to stick their noses into other people's business; it's a good way to get them cut off. Besides, you're a lot safer with me than you'd be with any of those bandits."

"Oh, really?" Her tone was laced with thick sarcasm.

"Really. As a general rule, I tend to prefer my women willing." His amber eyes scanned the room. "Unfortunately, several of these gentlemen aren't nearly so fastidious."

His words tolled a warning in Davina's head. She had been so bound and determined to succeed in this that she had refused to admit to the hazards involved in her expedition. Now she was forced to admit that she might have gotten herself in over her head before she had even begun. Realizing that he was telling the truth about his disreputable patrons, Davina decided that the only option open to her at the moment was to humor Sam McGee. To a point, she added silently.

"If I stay and drink Luis's damned margarita, will you let me go?"

He nodded. "Not only that, I'll walk you to your hotel."

The salt-rimmed glass had been on the way to her lips. At his words, she lowered it to the table. A bit of the icy liquid sloshed over the top of the glass.

"I'm certainly not staying here overnight."

He reached behind him, plucking a towel from an empty table and began casually mopping up the spilled drink. "Of course you are."

It had been necessary to release her in order to clean up the liquid. Realizing that she was suddenly free to leave, Davina began to stand.

"I wouldn't do that," he said laconically. "You've already managed to draw attention to yourself. If you walk out of here alone, little lady, I guarantee you're going to find yourself in more trouble than you bargained for."

"I've got to get to the plane," she insisted, growing frantic as she looked down at her watch.

At that moment, the steady drone of the old World War II cargo plane sounded overhead. "If that's the plane you're talking about—and it must be, because it's the only one in town—I think you've just missed it."

"Damn. Since when is anything ever on time in this country?" Frustrated, Davina took a drink of the margarita, finding it surprisingly good.

He leaned back in the chair and crossed his arms over his chest. "So now we can get down to business."

"I was mistaken about that," she ground out, irrationally hating his suddenly friendly smile. "I came to Calderitas to hire someone. I thought you were that man. It's obvious that you're not."

He reached for the bottle, then appeared to change his mind. "And you're quite an expert on men," he said quietly, lighting a cigarette instead. "What did you say about having experienced thousands?"

"Not 'experienced.' 'Studied.'"

He looked at her with renewed interest. "I'd heard college curriculums had changed since my time, but if it's possible to major in the opposite sex these days, I just might consider going back for an advanced degree."

The surprising knowledge that this uncouth man had any type of college degree was overshadowed by the idea that whatever his official field of study had been, Davina would bet her last nickel that women had been his specialty.

"I majored in anthropology," she said stiffly. "With an emphasis on Mesoamerican archaeology. And believe me, Mr. McGee, that macho attitude you've obviously worked so hard to perfect only demonstrates that some men have not evolved very far from the cave."

If he was offended by her accusation, Sam failed to reveal it. Instead, a flicker of wry amusement teased at the corners of his lips. "Do you know I once read that every woman should marry an archaeologist?"

"Really," she said in a tone of blatant boredom.

His grin was swift, bold and decidedly wicked. "Really. That way, the older she gets, the more interested he gets."

Davina shook her head, not bothering to conceal her frustration over the way this interview was turning out. "Don't you take anything seriously?"

"I certainly try not to."

"Mr. McGee—"

"Sam," he corrected.

Davina opted for middle ground. "Watch it, McGee," she warned. "You're in danger of becoming a stereotype."

He leaned forward and rested his arms on the table. "That's right, you're an expert on men, aren't you?"

"*Man*," she corrected. "I'm an expert on man. A bipedal primate mammal anatomically related to the great apes but distinguished primarily by notable brain development, with a resultant capacity for articulate speech and abstract reasoning."

"That's quite a mouthful," he said admiringly. "Is there one?"

"One what?"

"One man."

Unable to resist the temptation, he reached out, allowing his fingers to play with a strand of blond hair that had escaped the thick braid at the back of her neck. Unnerved by the intimate gesture, Davina jerked her head away.

Except for a slight narrowing of his eyes, Sam appeared unperturbed by her reaction. "Is there a man in your life, lovely—" His voice drifted off as he gave her a long look. "You haven't told me your name."

"There's no reason for you to know it," she insisted, "since we're obviously not going to be doing business."

"You know mine," he pointed out with whimsical logic.

Actually, her name had preceded her by a good three hours. News traveled fast in Calderitas, and an attractive blond American was not an everyday sight. But he didn't think Davina Lowell would enjoy knowing that she had succeeded in providing entertainment for an entire town.

Davina decided that the best way to escape this ridiculous situation was to humor him. "It's Davina. Davina Lowell."

She glanced at the half-empty bottle. How much more tequila would it take until he passed out, giving her the opportunity to ask Luis to walk her to the nearest hotel?

"Would you like another drink?" she asked sweetly.

Sam appeared not to have heard her question. "Davina," he said, as if trying the name out on his tongue. "Davina Lowell." He nodded. "Good New England name. Ancestors stepped right off the *Mayflower* onto Plymouth Rock. You've spent your entire life in a historic red brick house in Boston, except for summers at the Cape. Your father's a lawyer, your mother occupies her time by doing charity work.

"You have one sister. Younger," he decided after a slight pause, "who wants to be a social worker. Or a television personality.... Are you trying to get me drunk, Davina Lowell?"

"Not at all," she protested instantly, lying through her teeth. "And you're completely wrong about my family."

"That's okay. You can tell me your life story over breakfast in the morning. I'm glad you're not stupid enough to try to get me drunk, Davina, because it'd take more than what's left in this bottle to do the job. And since my shipment didn't arrive on that plane with you today, I should probably begin preserving the inventory. What's the job you're offering?"

"Do you really own this place?"

"Such as it is. Not exactly what you're used to, is it?"

"I don't spend a great deal of time in taverns."

"Now, why doesn't that surprise me? The job?" he prompted.

Davina took a second sip of her drink, finding it even better than the first. "This is good."

"Luis uses fresh limes; most places use a bottled mix. Are you through stalling?"

"I'm not stalling," she said angrily, annoyed that with time at such a premium, she had wasted so many days tracking down this man. First thing tomorrow morning she was going to search out the second prospect on her list.

Several pairs of dark eyes were regarding her with undisguised interest. Realizing that her outburst had once again drawn an audience, Davina lowered her voice. "I was informed that you were a guide."

"I used to be. Now I just hang around here, waiting for pretty American *turistas* to walk in the door."

Davina glanced around the interior of the decidedly rustic cantina. "I can't believe you get that many tourists."

"You're right. Most of the ones who look like you end up at Cancún." He studied her thoughtfully through the haze of blue cigarette smoke. "Actually, now that you mention it, all the ones who look like you end up at Cancún."

"You sound as if you're familiar with the place."

He shrugged carelessly, but Davina couldn't help noticing that his lips, which had been nearing a smile, were now pulled into a taut, grim line. "I used to spend some time there."

Despite her avowed lack of interest in Sam McGee, his gritty tone undeniably piqued her curiosity. Try as she might, she could not picture this disreputable individual in the glittering playground of the wealthy.

"Really? Did you own a tavern there, too?"

Sam ground out the cigarette in a shell masquerading as an ashtray, then splashed a generous amount of tequila into his glass. Tossing back his head, he swallowed it before answering.

"I was in a different line of work in those days. Now, if we're through with the obligatory getting-to-know-you chitchat, I'd like to get down to brass tacks. What's the job and what are you paying?"

Well, considering the amount of alcohol he had consumed just during the time she had been in the cantina, the man could certainly be coherent when he wanted to, Davina considered. She was beginning to realize that her initial impression might have been a bit hasty. Sam McGee appeared to be a more complex individual than he had seemed at first glance.

"I want to hike across the peninsula."

He had been in the process of refilling the glass, but at her words, he slammed the bottle down onto the table and stared at her. "Look, lady, if you're tired of the beaches on Cancún and want to move on to Acapulco, it's a helluva lot easier to fly there."

"It won't work. I need to hike it. And I need a guide. A sober one," she tacked on pointedly.

Ignoring her sarcasm, he poured another drink. "I must be drunker than I thought," he mused aloud. "You're a hallucination, right?" he asked hopefully.

"I'm not a hallucination. But you are drunk."

"Obviously not drunk enough," he muttered, fixing her with an irritated look. "So why don't you let me in on what possible reason a nice, properly brought-up lady like you could have to go marching around in that malarial jungle?"

Reminding herself that of the three men on her list, Sam McGee's rather sketchy credentials were the best suited to her purpose, Davina decided to give the man one last chance to redeem himself.

"I'm going to have to ask you to honor the secrecy of my expedition."

He seemed to be fighting back a smile as he viewed her sober expression. "Far be it from me to breathe a single word to a living soul."

Davina noted the sarcasm in his tone. "This is serious, Mr. McGee."

"You were going to drop the 'Mr.,' remember?" He lifted his right hand. "I promise, on my word as a former eagle scout, not to tell anyone about Ms Davina Lowell's top-secret expedition. There—does that make you feel any better?"

"You were an eagle scout?"

"Why do you find that so hard to believe? We were all young once."

Davina knew that. But a boy scout? Reform school, she mused, her gaze taking in his hard amber eyes and defiant, jutting jaw—now that, she just might accept.

"It doesn't really matter what I believe," she said finally. "The important thing is that you give me your word."

"You have it."

She inclined her head in a brief, formal nod. "Thank you."

"Of course you'll have to decide for yourself whether or not my word is worth anything."

Once again Davina asked herself why she was even considering telling this man about her plan. It was obvious they would never be able to work together. An expedition such as this needed one person in charge. She couldn't imagine Sam McGee ever taking orders from anyone, let alone a woman.

"You may be unprincipled, but you're just old-fashioned enough to believe that a man's word means something," Davina decided after a long, thoughtful pause.

As Sam leaned back in his chair once again, his lips quirked. "Thanks—I think," he said dryly. "So now that I've promised to keep your secret, why don't you tell me about this mysterious quest."

Davina took a deep breath. She had only stated her purpose aloud to one person: Brad. Expecting enthusiastic support from the man she expected to marry someday, Davina had been more than a little hurt when he had practically laughed her out of his office.

"I'm going to find Naj Taxim."

The chair legs hit the floor with a resounding crash. "You *are* kidding."

She shook her head. "Not at all."

His tawny eyes narrowed consideringly. "I thought you claimed to be an educated woman."

"I am. In fact, I'm the third generation of Lowells to receive my doctorate before my twenty-third birthday," she added proudly.

"Congratulations. So how old are you now?"

"I'll be thirty-one in September. However, I don't see what my age has to do with anything."

"I was just wondering how long it took a Lowell to garner any common sense," he drawled. "I guess you're late bloomers, huh?"

Davina frowned. "You don't have to be so nasty. If you don't want to take me to Naj Taxim, just say so."

"I don't want to take you to Naj Taxim."

"Well, I suppose that leaves me with Alexander Morrison."

"Morrison?" Sam growled, suddenly alert.

"That's right. He's the second man on my list. I'm sure *he* won't be afraid to guide me across the peninsula—especially when it means getting his name in all the history books."

"Morrison would have to be able to read to give two hoots in hell about that," Sam shot back. "And for your information, lady, I'm damn well not afraid."

"That's what you say," she accused sweetly. "But it's a moot point, isn't it? Since by this time tomorrow I'll be in Veracruz, hiring Mr. Morrison to guide me to the legendary lost city of the Maya."

"You'll have to wait a few days."

"Why?"

"For Morrison to get out of jail."

Davina felt her heart sink to the sawdust-covered floor. "Jail?"

"Jail."

"I don't suppose you know what the charges are?" she asked hopefully.

"He got in a fight."

"Oh." Davina felt immensely relieved. From what she had seen of this part of the country thus far, that was standard operating procedure.

"With the woman he lives with," Sam tacked on significantly.

There was a long pause while Davina considered the implications of that statement. "Oh."

"Oh," Sam mimicked. "Is that all you can say?"

"The woman," Davina ventured tentatively, "was she hurt?"

He shrugged. "A black eye, some bruises, couple of cracked ribs. Oh, and I heard she lost her two front teeth in the scuffle."

"That's an obscene way to treat a woman!" Davina was truly aghast at his words.

"Why don't you tell that to Morrison when you're alone out in the jungle with him," he suggested in a bland, uncaring tone.

Davina had had more than enough of Sam McGee's mocking attitude. "I just may do that," she snapped, rising from the table to march toward the door. On her way out of the cantina, she stopped briefly at the bar.

"Thank you for the margarita, Luis," she said with a genuine smile. "It was the best I've ever had."

The young man seemed embarrassed by her words of praise, but smiled nonetheless. A moment later, a husky roadblock, dressed in the garb of a French merchant marine, appeared in her way.

"Don't be in such a hurry to leave, *chérie*," the man drawled drunkenly. "Why don't you and I go for a little stroll and get better acquainted?" Gray eyes the color of cold steel roved from the top of her head down to her feet. Davina felt goose bumps rise on her arms.

"I'm sorry," she protested, trying to move around the obstruction, "but I don't think that would be such a good idea."

He grabbed her arm as she attempted to pass. "Have a drink while you think it over." His smile was nothing less than a leer. "Luis, my man," he called out, " a drink for the lady."

The sailor's arm was the circumference of a tree trunk, making escape impossible as he pulled Davina against him. "We don't get many blondes in Calderitas," he said, dispatching the tie at the end of her braid with a single, deft movement. His thick fingers wove harshly through the intricate braiding, releasing lush waves that rippled over her shoulders. "You'll be a nice change."

He said something in rapid-fire French that had the men seated at the bar laughing uproariously. Davina could tell she would be getting no help from that quarter. Her desperate eyes darted to the table at the back of the cantina. It was deserted.

"Please, I really have to go." She hated to beg, but at this point, Davina wasn't going to worry about false pride—not when so much more was at stake.

Ignoring her request, the sailor took the drink Luis reluctantly placed on the bar. "Here," he sneered, lifting it to her tightly shut lips, "you need to relax. One of Luis's margaritas will loosen you up so we can have ourselves a fun party."

As he tipped the glass, the icy liquid ran down her chin and onto the front of her blouse. The man swore a string of virulent oaths.

"I said, drink," he growled, his hand tangling in her hair as he pushed the glass against her lips.

As his steely eyes dropped to the stain darkening the material over her breasts, Davina decided to fight, whatever the consequences. The man's intentions were obvious; she had nothing to lose.

Saying a small mental prayer, she took a deep breath and prepared to make her move.

2

"THE LADY has already had a drink."

Despite her earlier irritation with Sam McGee, Davina was admittedly relieved to hear the sound of the familiar, gritty voice.

"So?" the French sailor challenged. "Since when is there any law against her having another? It's not like you to turn down business, McGee."

The icy liquid sloshed onto the floor as he swayed, appearing dangerously close to passing out. "Luis, a pitcher of your famous margaritas for the lady and a bottle of absinthe for me. We're going to have ourselves a little party." His arm curled around Davina's waist.

"I'm afraid you've misunderstood the situation, Raoul," Sam said to the Frenchman in that low, dangerous tone he had used when ordering Davina to stay at the table. "Ms Lowell is with me."

The man's enormous hands instantly fell away, as if burned. The margarita dropped unheeded to the floor, darkening the sawdust underfoot. "Hey, Sam," he protested, backing away, holding his palms in front of him as if for protection, "I did not mean anything. I had no way of knowing that you had already staked your claim."

"Now you do." Although Sam's tone remained soft, almost amiable, his tawny eyes were as hard as agate. He returned his attention to Davina. "Ready to go, sweetheart?"

Her initial fear was metamorphosing into a slow, simmering rage as she realized that the sailor was not apologizing to her, but to Sam. More than anything, she wanted to tell the smugly self-satisfied man that she didn't want his assistance; that she didn't need it.

But she could feel the interested stares of the cantina's patrons and knew that Sam had been right about one thing: Raoul was merely an example of the trouble a woman could find herself in by entering a waterfront tavern unescorted.

"Ready," she said through clenched teeth.

Sam looped a friendly arm around her shoulder. "That's my girl," he said with a bold, reckless grin. "I knew such an intelligent, overeducated woman couldn't keep acting like a prize jackass all day."

Davina gave him a blistering glare as they crossed the room. "I'm perfectly capable of taking care of myself, Mr. McGee."

"Yeah, I saw how capable you are."

"I'll have you know that I have a black belt in karate," she insisted. "I can break bricks with my bare hands."

"Of course you can," he stated easily. "That's why you had everything under control back there. I could tell poor Raoul was trembling in his boots."

Her eyes shot furious sparks. While her name might not garner instant recognition, as was the case with her father's, Davina Lowell was accustomed to being taken seriously.

"Has anyone ever told you that you're an arrogant, egotistical, insufferable bastard?"

Sam half smiled. "All the time," he answered. "And while it's a helluva tough reputation to maintain, I try my best to live up to the image."

"You're crazy," she said tightly as they walked out into the blazing sun. "Everyone in this damn town is crazy. It must be something in the water." Her stomach suddenly lurched as a thought occurred to her.

"What's the matter now?" he asked, looking down at her suddenly stricken expression.

"The water," Davina said. "Damn, I didn't even think."

He dismissed her concern. "Oh, is that all?"

Damn the man! It was all his fault. If he hadn't gotten her so unsettled, she wouldn't have made such a careless, foolish mistake in the first place.

"It's easy for you to take such a blasé attitude," she shot back. "Since it's undoubtedly been years since anything unfermented has passed those lips. And even if it did, the alcohol level in your body would kill any parasites that had the nerve to try to settle in. Unfortunately I haven't spent the past five years pickling my insides."

Sam was both surprised and disturbed that Davina knew how long he had been in the Yucatán. Apparently he had not covered his tracks as well as he'd thought. It took a Herculean effort, but he managed to keep his voice nonchalant.

"You know about me."

"A bit," she acknowledged. "I did my homework before flying down here, but I wasn't able to learn a great deal—only that you arrived here in Calderitas from the States five years ago and bought a deep-sea fishing boat. While your business is reasonably successful, you don't make as much money from the venture as you might because you steadfastly refuse to ply the potential tourist trade.

"You've hiked every inch of this part of the country and know it like the back of your hand. If the price is right, you've been known to hire out as a guide, mostly for mining and petroleum engineers searching for new fields. I didn't know about the cantina."

"That's a fairly recent acquisition," he said absently, his thoughts on the information she had unearthed. What else had she managed to find out about him? "I won it in a poker game a few months ago. That's quite a bit of information you've dug up. I didn't realize I had such a reputation."

Sam didn't like discovering that he wasn't as anonymous as he had thought. Five years ago he had left the States for the Yucatán, leaving no forwarding address. To the rest of the world, it appeared Sam McGee had dropped off the face of the earth. He had his own reasons for wanting to keep it that way.

"They say there's no man alive in Mexico who knows the peninsula like you do." Her voice held a reluctant admiration.

"They exaggerate."

Davina knew that what she was doing could well be considered foolhardy. In fact, she mused, if her fellow faculty members knew what she was doing during her vacation, they would probably all be stunned by her rash, atypical and highly unprofessional behavior.

As it was, everyone with the exception of Brad thought she was basking on the pristine beaches of Cancún. Although she had felt guilty about lying to them, Davina had decided it was definitely preferable to present them with a fait accompli. After all, everyone else concerned with her father's disappearance, including the Mexican *federales*, believed that Jordan Lowell was dead. Only Davina refused to give up hope. If her father was alive, she was going to find him.

"Were you telling the truth about Alexander Morrison?" she asked suddenly.

"Not exactly."

Davina nodded knowingly. "I thought as much."

"I left out the rough parts because I didn't want to risk offending your delicate sensibilities."

For some strange reason, Davina believed him. "I suppose I'm down to Ryder Long."

"Good choice," Sam said amiably as he stopped in front of a two-story frame structure.

The weathered gray building wasn't really a hotel—at least not the kind Ms Davina Lowell was undoubtedly accustomed to. But Molly McGuire ran a tight ship; she didn't allow fighting or excessive drinking in her boardinghouse. And Sam knew that if he asked, she'd keep a close eye on this dizzy broad who appeared to have more good looks than common sense.

"I'm relieved you finally agree with something," Davina murmured dryly. She glanced curiously over his shoulder. "Is this the hotel?"

"It's where you're staying."

She stifled a frustrated sigh. "I suppose I have no other choice but to stay here tonight. Tomorrow I'll fly north and contact Mr. Long."

"Whatever you want," he agreed amiably. "In fact, I'll even write you a letter of introduction."

"Let me get this straight," Davina said, suspicious about his suddenly congenial attitude. "Are you recommending Mr. Long for the job?"

"I think he'll be terrific. So far as I know, he hasn't raped a woman for two, maybe three, weeks," he said as he led her up the steps of the veranda.

"Oh, and by the way, the water was bottled. I may be a bastard, but I do stop at giving Montezuma's revenge to a lady." He opened the door, gesturing Davina into the rooming house.

"Sammy! It's been too long!"

A tall woman of Rubenesque proportions, clad in a scarlet silk kimono, wrapped her arms around Sam as he entered the front room. Lush auburn hair the color of mahogany trailed down her back as she tilted her head to smile up at him. "I was beginning to think you'd been avoiding me."

"I've been a little busy."

She nodded. "So I hear. The word is that you're actually making Mick's old place turn a profit."

He shrugged. "It's not much, but we managed to catch up what Mick owed—as well as paying our liquor bills last month."

Her brown eyes held merriment. "If you don't watch out, Sammy, my boyo, you'll find yourself back in that same old rat race."

Sam damned the time he'd gotten drunk and told Molly about his life before Calderitas. Even though she was a good and trustworthy soul, he was decidedly uncomfortable with anyone knowing his secrets.

"I've got a slight problem," he said, ignoring her playful warning about his business.

Molly turned her interested gaze to Davina, who had been silently witnessing the exchange between Sam and this extraordinary woman, whose age Davina guessed to be somewhere between fifty and seventy. Davina noted with interest that Sam's expression had relaxed. His smile was genuine, and honest affection had softened the hard amber of his eyes to gleaming gold. She couldn't help but be intrigued by the warmth of those eyes.

"So I see," Molly murmured. Her eyes observed Davina shrewdly as she held out a plump, beringed hand. "Since Sammy here has forgotten his manners, as usual, I suppose it's up to us to introduce ourselves. I'm Molly. And as the sign outside states, this is my place."

Davina succumbed to the warmth in the woman's greeting, relaxing for the first time since her arrival in Calderitas. "Davina Lowell," she said as she allowed her hand to disappear into Molly's fleshy but surprisingly strong one.

"She needs a room for the night."

Molly's gaze went from Davina to Sam and back again. "I see."

Realizing that Molly was about to jump to the wrong conclusion, Sam hurried to explain. "She's looking for a guide."

"It appears you've found yourself one," Molly said to Davina.

"Actually, there are two other men I want to interview before making a final decision," Davina insisted quickly. "I'm only here in Calderitas tonight because I missed the plane out of town."

She didn't think it wise to explain that there was absolutely no way she was going to put her future, not to mention her father's life, in the hands of Sam McGee. Not after what she had seen of him this afternoon. However, if even half of what Sam had told her was true, her other two prospects weren't so promising, either.

Molly looked unconvinced, but appeared to accept Davina's answer for the time being. "Well, we're a bit crowded right now, with the *Orgueil de Toulon* in port." She chewed thoughtfully on a burgundy-tinted fingernail. "I know," she said suddenly, her expression brightening, "you can bunk with Annie."

"I wouldn't want to put anyone out," Davina protested.

Molly was obviously amused by her guest's polite demeanor. "Hell's bells, honey—forgive my French—you won't be putting her out. Annie's my brother's girl; she's been staying here while he's out to sea."

She chuckled throatily. "At least she's supposed to be staying with me. Ever since she fell in love with that young man down at the telegraph office, she's only been home long enough to change clothes." Her broad, womanly smile was contagious. "No sense in a bed sitting there empty—that's what I always say."

Davina rose several notches in Sam's unwilling esteem as she gave Molly a warm, nonjudgmental smile. "It's very nice of you to take me in like this."

"Shoot, sweetheart," Molly protested, "any friend of Sammy's is a friend of mine." She looked around. "Where's your gear?"

"It's back at the airstrip," Davina said. "The baggage handler assured me that he'd take care of it until I returned."

Molly and Sam exchanged a long look. "Hell," Sam groaned, dragging his hand over his face, "I guess it's up to me."

"Of course it is," Molly responded without missing a beat. "After all, it's obvious that your friend here could use a little nap." The woman's alert eyes skimmed over Davina. "No offense, honey, but you're beginning to look like something the cat dragged in."

"It's only jet lag," Davina assured her, brushing a few strands of hair back from her sticky forehead. "Plus the change in temperature. It'll just take me a little time to adjust."

Davina turned her attention to Sam. "I appreciate your help, Mr. McGee," she said politely. "Please don't worry about my luggage. I'll retrieve it once I wash up and get my bearings. After all, I left it in good hands."

"You sure as hell did. Manuel's got the fastest hands in Calderitas."

"Sam, don't pick on the poor girl so," Molly advised quietly. "How was she supposed to know?"

"If she had half the sense God gave a mushroom, she would have figured it out for herself," he ground out.

Davina didn't appreciate the way they were talking about her as if she weren't even in the room. "Figured what out?"

As her questioning gaze went back and forth between Molly's openly sympathetic expression and Sam's frustrated one, Davina began to suffer a grave misgiving.

"Oh, no," she groaned. "Manuel doesn't work for the airline, does he?"

Sam regarded her coolly. "Got it on the first try. How reassuring to discover that all that money your parents spent on your education wasn't a total waste."

"You don't have to be sarcastic, Mr. McGee," Davina snapped, feeling ridiculously foolish. "Anyone can make a mistake."

"Yeah, but why was I unlucky enough to get the job of fixing up yours?"

"You've already done more than enough by finding me a place to stay the night," Davina said seriously. "I'll simply explain to Manuel that my luggage contains important papers and journals necessary for my work. I'm certain I can make him understand the seriousness of the situation."

Sam rolled his eyes toward the ceiling. "Deliver me from Pollyanna." He returned his attention to Molly, who had been watching the exchange with amused interest. "Keep an eye on her while I'm gone," he instructed. "The lady definitely needs a keeper."

As Davina began to bristle dangerously, Molly placed a restraining hand on the younger woman's arm. "Don't worry about a thing, Sammy," she assured him. "We'll get along just fine."

Sam looked decidedly dubious about Molly's ability to keep her visitor out of further trouble, but didn't bother to argue the point. "Stay put," he instructed Davina gruffly. "I'll be back to take you to dinner around nine."

"That certainly isn't necessary."

He swore. "Do you always argue every little point? Would it really kill you to keep your mouth shut for once in your life?"

Davina had had more than enough of his overbearing attitude. Lifting her chin, she met his derisive gaze with a challenging one of her own.

"I've no intention of going out with you, Mr. McGee. Despite my interest in lost civilizations, Neanderthals have never held any vast appeal for me!"

"Davina, dear," Molly cut in swiftly, coaxingly, "perhaps you'd enjoy a nice, cool bath."

Sam's glare could have cut diamonds. "Relax, sweetheart, I wasn't asking for a date. You're in need of a guide, right?"

"That's correct, but—"

"As you so accurately pointed out, I happen to be the best. I figure the least I can do is to hear this cockeyed plan of yours and since we both have to eat, it only makes sense to save time and discuss it over dinner."

Davina was both angered by his acid tone and embarrassed by the idea that she had once again jumped to the wrong conclusion. She inclined her head briefly, formally.

"That's not a bad idea," she admitted reluctantly. "However, I insist on paying for my own meal."

Sam decided that if he didn't get out of here soon, he'd be tempted to wring her lissome neck. He'd never met a more argumentative female. Once again he found himself conjecturing about whether Davina Lowell was involved with some guy back in the States. If so, Sam's heart went out to the poor bastard; this was one female who could drive a man to drink.

"Don't let her out of your sight," he instructed Molly brusquely. Not trusting himself to say anything else to

Davina, he turned on his heel and strode from the room. A
moment later the screen door slammed.

"Let's get you settled in," Molly said cheerfully, blithely
ignoring Sam's display of temper. "You'll want a bath, I
suspect. And something light to eat. And a nap."

"It all sounds wonderful," Davina said wistfully. "This is
very nice of you, Molly." Though she was unused to such
informality on first meeting, Davina belatedly realized that
she had never been given the ebullient woman's last name.

"Hell, honey, I'm just doing what Sammy instructed—
looking after you. Something tells me that you're in for a
very long night. The least I can do is make certain that
you're well prepared."

With that less-than-encouraging statement, Molly looped
a fleshy arm around Davina's shoulders and led her up the
stairs.

AFTER A COOLING BATH, a light repast of fresh fruit and a
nap, Davina felt renewed, ready to face anything. Later,
however, as she sat across the table from Sam in the cantina, she wondered if she had been overly optimistic. He was
more amiable than earlier in the day but no less domineer-
ing.

He had practically dragged her from Molly's and despite
her assurances that she was a grown woman, capable of
making her own decisions, he had insisted on ordering dinner for her.

In a way, Davina was glad for the opportunity to watch
Sam in action. It proved what she had already suspected—
she could no more trek through the jungle with this man
than she could fly to the moon.

"I suppose I should thank you for retrieving my luggage," she said as she sipped on the margarita Sam had imperiously ordered for her.

His wide shoulders lifted in a careless shrug. "Someone had to do it." From his tone, Davina detected that he wished it had been someone—anyone—else.

"It was still a very thoughtful thing to do. Did Manuel give you any trouble?" she asked as an afterthought.

"Nah. I did just like you suggested."

"I suggested?"

"I merely explained the importance of your work."

"And he understood?"

"Let's just say Manuel saw the light," Sam drawled. As he lifted his own glass to his lips, Davina saw dark purple bruises discoloring his skinned knuckles.

"You didn't hit him?"

Slowly, with deliberate patience, Sam lowered his drink to the table. "Lady, you've got your precious stuff back. Why quibble about how it was done?"

Davina didn't like his patronizing tone. "Because I didn't ask you to help me in the first place," she returned heatedly. "And if I had, I certainly wouldn't have wanted you to beat the poor man up!"

An incredulous look moved over his face. "There you go with that 'poor man' stuff again. Did you bother to take a good look at your bogus baggage-man when you were handing all your worldly possessions over to him?"

Remembering the massive bulk of the man she had foolishly mistaken for a baggage handler, Davina had the good grace to flush guiltily. "Were you hurt?"

"Now she asks," Sam muttered, more to himself than to Davina.

Davina decided that this interview was going no better than the earlier one. She was about to give up entirely when Sam fixed her with an intent stare.

"What's the real reason behind this urge of yours to explore the peninsula?" he asked suddenly.

"I told you; I want to uncover Naj Taxim."

He shook his head. "Uh-uh. That isn't going to cut it, Davina Lowell. Why don't you try giving me the straight story this time?"

"I am giving you the straight story." As he continued to give her that intent, knowing stare, Davina's throat went unreasonably dry. She swallowed.

"All right," she admitted finally. "There is another reason."

"I thought so."

"I'm searching for my father."

"Your father."

"That's right. He's been missing for the past fifteen months. Everyone—the authorities, the people he works with, his friends—all believe he's dead."

"And you don't."

"My father and I were very close. If he were dead, I'd know it." She shook her head forcefully. "I know he's alive somewhere out there. Just as I know he's found Naj Taxim."

Sam found himself unreasonably affected by her earnest expression. "Why do you think he's found the one place men have been seeking for centuries?"

"Because he's one of the world's leading authorities on the Maya, and Naj Taxim was his obsession. The fact that he didn't return from his last trip to look for the city proves he's located it. I'm afraid that he's being held captive by the people living there."

"I'll say this for you, sweetheart, you've got one hell of an imagination." Before she could respond, something clicked in the back of Sam's mind—something unbidden and decidedly unwelcome.

"What's your father's name?"

"Jordan Lowell. Have you heard of him?" Davina asked hopefully.

"We may not be the hub of civilization, Ms Lowell," he countered, "but even in Calderitas, the name Jordan Lowell garners its share of recognition."

Damn. As he felt the heavy mantle of responsibility settling down over his shoulders, Sam wondered why he hadn't made the connection before. It must have been the tequila, he decided. In a futile attempt to forget the events of five years ago, he had numbed his brain just enough to block out the name of the one man he could never, under normal circumstances, forget.

Sam didn't believe Davina Lowell's farfetched story about Naj Taxim. He didn't even believe Jordan Lowell was alive. Before shifting his interest to cultural anthropology—specifically the discovery of lost tribes—the scientist had developed a world-renowned reputation as a brilliant archaeologist. Sam doubted that there were any ruins left anywhere in the world that Davina's father had not explored. The man was a veteran explorer; skilled in jungle survival. If he were indeed alive, he would have made his appearance known long ago. But Davina believed her father to be alive. And until she had been proved wrong, the woman was just stubborn enough to keep looking for him.

At that moment, Luis suddenly appeared beside the table with their dinner, giving Sam a much-needed respite from this conversation. He needed time to think, to figure out what in the hell he was going to do about Davina's absurd quest.

Luis remained silent as he placed the steaming plates on the table, quickly escaping what he obviously perceived to be the starting battleground of World War III.

"Eat your dinner before it gets cold," Sam instructed gruffly, waving his fork toward her plate. "Then we'll talk."

Davina was growing extremely tired of his overbearing behavior but, seduced by the tempting aroma, she turned her attention toward her meal.

"It smells delicious," she admitted. "What is it?"

"*Huachinango à la veracruzana.* Red snapper, Veracruz style," Sam translated with a rare, genuine smile. "I think you'll like it."

Davina had already determined that Sam did not give away many smiles. As she felt herself succumbing to its warmth, she was strangely relieved that such occasions were few and far between. There were times, albeit fleeting, when the man could appear almost handsome, in a rough-hewn sort of way. When the craggy lines of his face softened inexplicably, when his tawny eyes warmed to sparkling gold and his teeth flashed white against bronze skin darkened even further by several days' growth of beard, Sam McGee was strangely, strikingly appealing.

"If it tastes anything like it smells, I'll love it," she agreed quietly, dropping her eyes to her plate to keep him from seeing her confusion.

Fortunately Sam appeared much more interested in his meal than in Davina's strange reaction to his sudden good humor. She was undeniably relieved as he allowed her to sample the exquisitely prepared fish, rice and corn in silence.

3

LATER, OVER CUPS of rich, dark coffee, Sam returned the conversation to Davina's reason for being in Calderitas.

"So the lady has an urge to explore the jungle." He plucked an orange from the basket of fruit Luis had placed on the table after removing their dinner plates.

"That's right."

He had nice hands, Davina considered irrelevantly as she watched him peel the fruit. Strong, wide, with long fingers and square-cut nails. For a fleeting moment she wondered what those hands would feel like on her body. Shaking her head with dismay at her errant fantasy, Davina vowed to stay away from Luis's margaritas. As she was unaccustomed to liquor, the alcohol had obviously gone to her head.

"In order to find Naj Taxim, the fabled lost city of the Maya," Sam continued. Intent on peeling the orange, he missed the blatant desire that had flashed across her face. "And let's not forget your missing father, the world-famous archaeologist, Jordan Lowell."

Davina nodded. "Right again."

He dug his thumbnail between two segments of the now-peeled fruit. "Want a piece?"

"Thank you." She accepted the slice of orange, relishing the explosion of its sweetness in her mouth. "It's delicious."

"Veracruz supplies the rest of the country with most of its fruit." Sam leaned back in his chair and fixed her with a half smile. "You know," he said conversationally, "I've spent all afternoon and evening trying to decide whether you're certifiably crazy or if you've just spent too much time out in our Mexican sun."

So he really wasn't going to take her seriously after all. Davina wondered why she had thought he might. She stood up. "How much do I owe you for dinner?"

"Sit down," he said with a sigh. "As for dinner, it's on the house."

"I always pay my debts, Mr. McGee."

"Fine. So pay for your supper by telling me why you believe Naj Taxim is anything more than a myth."

Davina eyed him suspiciously. "Why should you care what I believe? It's obvious that you've already made up your mind."

"Let's just say you've piqued my interest, sweetheart." He motioned toward her abandoned chair.

Secretly needing to talk to someone—anyone—about her plan, Davina sat down. "It's a long story."

"I've got nothing else pressing to do at the moment." His tone was faintly amused.

"Do you promise that you'll withhold judgment until I've finished?"

"Why don't you just start at the beginning?"

"I'm an associate professor of archaeology, specializing in Mesoamerican cultures."

"Where?"

"Boston University."

"It figures."

"What figures?" She could hear the edge of sarcasm in his voice, but was unable to discern its meaning.

"The clothes," he pointed out. "I should have recognized that skirt; all it lacks is the obligatory alligator stamped on your backside." His tawny eyes swept over her dismissingly. "Aren't you a little old for the pretty look, Ms Lowell?"

"If you're going to insult me, I'm leaving," she warned.

"Go ahead." Sam's gaze shifted to the doorway. "Raoul just showed up again; perhaps you can sweet-talk him into walking you back to Molly's."

"You're despicable," Davina said through clenched teeth.

Sam's only response was an uncaring shrug. "So you keep telling me. Continue on with your story," he suggested as he lit a cigarette.

Her expelled sigh ruffled her bangs. She'd come too far to give up now, Davina reminded herself. And as unattractive as the prospect was, right now Sam McGee was the only thing she had going for her.

"My father is on staff at Harvard. Two years ago, he received a letter."

"Stating the existence of a secret map to the lost city of the Maya."

She looked at him in surprise. "Why, that's right. How did you know?"

He drew in on the cigarette. "Lucky guess. What did he do?"

"At first, he thought it was a joke—or at best a less-than-subtle scam. We both did; Brad, too."

"Brad?"

"Bradford Stevenson, my father's assistant. Actually," she elaborated, "Brad is beginning to develop quite a reputation of his own in academic circles. His paper on Toltec fetishes was quite well received."

"Good for old Brad," Sam responded dryly. "I take it Stevenson doesn't agree with your theory about Naj Taxim."

"Not really," Davina admitted, looking down at the table.

Sam watched her hands twist together in her lap. He was obviously venturing into sensitive conversational territory, but if he did end up going along with Davina Lowell's harebrained scheme, he didn't want to run into any surprises along the way. Like a jealous protégé—or lover—he suddenly wondered exactly how close a relationship Davina had with her father's assistant.

"He also doesn't believe the old man's still alive."

Davina lifted her eyes to meet his. "No."

Sam would have had to have been blind to miss the shadow that passed over those unique blue-green eyes. Old Brad had obviously let her down. Sam wondered why he should even care that the guy had hurt her. He shook off the atypical feeling of sympathy.

"What happened to change your father's mind?"

"I didn't know at first," she admitted. "My father was a very busy man. He didn't have time to share all the details of his work with me. But something certainly happened to change his mind—something so important that he left before the end of the term."

She managed a slight smile. "Actually, according to Brad, the administration was livid. But not only is my father tenured, he brings the university a great deal of prestige, so there wasn't much they could do."

The sad little smile moved to her eyes. "I know what you're probably thinking," she said. "And you're right: Daddy is a prima donna. But he's my father. And I love him."

Sam studied her intent face. Actually, when she wasn't arguing, Davina Lowell was a decidedly lovely woman. Not beautiful—at least not in the traditional sense of the word—but when her face was lit with enthusiasm, as it was now, she possessed an inner glow that made her skin gleam like pearls. And the intelligence in her soft-turquoise eyes added a dimension he was unused to seeing in the women of his acquaintance.

While the cotton skirt and prim white blouse she was wearing were decidedly asexual, they couldn't entirely hide a figure that, although a little skinny for his taste, at least had curves in all the right places. All in all, Sam decided, a man could do a helluva lot worse. He wondered if she would show the same enthusiasm she felt for her work in bed, and decided that with the right man, she just might.

He felt her looking at him curiously and realized he'd been lost in his own erotic thoughts. "You were telling me what changed your father's mind," Sam said, reluctantly returning his mind to the conversation at hand.

Davina leaned forward, her eyes sparkling with an inner excitement that, if they had been talking about anything else, would have served to further his sensual fantasies.

"He found proof of the city's existence."

Sam calculated roughly how many times in the past five years he had heard a similar story: hundreds, at least.

The legend of Naj Taxim was an evocative one, hinting at a secret city of gold, the final palaces belonging to a dwindling civilization and erected before the jungle had reclaimed its own and the Maya had all but vanished. The search for Naj Taxim had been going on for centuries. First the Spanish conquistadors had sought it, followed in turn by treasure seekers from every corner of the globe. The archaeologists came in to the Yucatán in droves, seeking a treasure that transcended the rumored bounty of gold, jade and precious jewels.

Naj Taxim made the kind of story a man liked to contemplate while alone in the dark recesses of the jungle on a starry night. Sam had certainly thought about the lost city on such occasions. But it was sheer fantasy—as ethereal as moonlight, as unreachable as a star.

He didn't want to begin to guess how many more wide-eyed optimistic fools would arrive in the Yucatán, clutching maps promising fame and fortune, before the world ran out of suckers.

Davina's words broke into his thoughts. "The map is authentic," she stated firmly. "I know it is."

"Yeah, just as authentic as the map to Atlantis the jerk sold some other mark last week. And don't forget the one for the Seven Cities of Cibola. Not to mention the one and only map to the Lost Dutchman's Mine. I hear he has those printed up by the thousands."

"You're a cynic, Mr. McGee."

He lifted his glass in acknowledgment. "And you're a fool, Ms Lowell."

She lowered her eyes to the table. "Since you think so little of me, it's probably best that we won't be working together," she said in an oddly disappointed tone.

There was something undeniably appealing about the woman when she allowed these fleeting glimpses of vulnerability. It was almost enough to make a man want to take care of her, protect her. Not wanting to ever be responsible for another living soul, Sam shook his head to clear it of that undesirable thought.

"You can't really intend to go through with this half-baked idea."

"Of course I do. And excuse me if I don't think rescuing my father is a half-baked idea," she retorted.

His expression softened. The change was almost imperceptible, but there was no mistaking the genuine sympathy Davina suddenly saw in his eyes.

"Look, I understand your concern; I also can see why the idea of your father's death would be a difficult one to accept. But—"

"He's not dead," Davina insisted firmly.

"You can't know that for sure. The jungle has a way of keeping its secrets."

Her eyes met his strangely sympathetic ones calmly, levelly. "If my father were dead, not only would I know it, I would accept that fact, as well. But he's not, Mr. McGee. He's somewhere out there and I'm going to find him."

"The same way you're going to find Naj Taxim."

Davina refused to react to the scorn in his tone. "I happen to have done some investigative work of my own and found in my father's office an ancient manuscript referring to the existence of the map; along with a list of everyone he had corresponded with concerning Naj Taxim. The list turned out to be even more extensive than I'd first thought, so I ended up sending out hundreds of letters of my own.

"Last month I received a letter from an individual who said he had heard about my search. He also claimed to be the man I'm looking for—the man who sold my father a map to the city a little more than fifteen months ago, right before his disappearance. Obviously that's what brought him down here."

She took a deep breath before continuing. "Don't you see, Sam? All I have to do is get my hands on that map and I'll know where to find him."

It did not escape his notice that in her enthusiasm, Davina had forgotten to maintain the distance of formality. She'd called him Sam. For some inexplicable reason he found himself liking what her throaty voice did with his less-than-lyrical name.

"How much did it cost you?" he asked wearily. He hoped that Davina was wealthy enough to be able to shrug off a few hundred lost dollars. The academic world was not known for its high salaries.

"A five-thousand-dollar down payment with the remainder due when I meet my contact at Chichén Itzá."

Sam stared at her. "Five thousand dollars?"

Davina nodded. "That was the down payment. I still owe him five thousand more."

Sam was struck with the sudden thought that Davina was actually carrying all that money around on her. She was lucky to still be alive. He considered that whoever had perpetrated the hoax on first Jordan Lowell, then his daughter, probably wouldn't bother sticking around to get the second half of the payoff.

Still, if the guy was from around here, there was a chance he knew him. One thing about running a cantina in this part of the world was that every crook, con man and renegade in the peninsula came through that door sooner or later.

"What's the name of your illustrious map salesman?" he asked suddenly.

"I don't exactly know," Davina admitted reluctantly. "The name he used in the letter turned out to be an alias."

Sam wasn't at all surprised by that little revelation. "Lady, you've got *chump* written all over you. When are you going to accept the fact that you and your father got conned, pure and simple?"

"I know the city exists; my father's manuscript describes it down to the last stone. Now all I need is the map."

"And if you don't get it?"

"I will." Davina could not—would not—allow herself to believe otherwise.

"You realize, of course, that your ancient manuscript could be a phony. Like your alleged map."

"I've had it examined," she argued. "It's dated 1519, and all the tests I've had done on the paper corroborate that fact. Have you ever heard of Gonzalo Guerrero?"

Sam shook a cigarette from a pack on the table. "It doesn't ring a bell. Is that the name your crooked map salesman goes by?"

Davina decided to ignore his sarcasm for the sake of a truce, no matter how tenuous. "Guerrero was a Spaniard. He and another Spaniard, a lay brother, Geronimo de Aguilar, survived a shipwreck off the coast in 1511."

A spiral of blue smoke rose to the ceiling as Sam lit the cigarette. "I suppose this little tale of derring-do is documented."

She nodded firmly, her tilted jaw daring him to challenge the validity of her story. "It certainly is. By several unimpeachable sources."

Sam decided he rather liked the way Davina could look so serious about her work. It had been a long time since he'd met anyone who had a true sense of dedication. Actually, now that he thought about it, the last individual he'd met with that character trait was Jordan Lowell. Like father, like daughter, he mused. Both were single-minded, stubborn dreamers. And this latest stunt proved they were both as crazy as hell.

"I believe you," he said simply.

Davina was surprised by his easy acceptance. She continued her story hesitantly, vaguely waiting for a renewed argument. "Anyway, the men had been serving the Maya as slaves when Hernán Cortés learned of them and hired Aguilar on as an interpreter in the Aztec conquest."

He drew in on the cigarette. "What happened to Guerrero?"

As she leaned toward him, Davina's eyes gleamed like gems. "That's the fascinating part. It turned out that he'd married a Mayan woman and converted. His body had been painted in the Mayan tradition and his ears mutilated. He had also cut his tongue in sacrificial fashion."

"Sounds like a charming fellow," he murmured dryly. "Is he the one who wrote your treasured paper?"

"No. Although several Spanish chroniclers documented Guerrero's conversion, it was Pedro de Alvarado who told about the founding of Naj Taxim. You see, Guerrero became especially famous after defying Montejo."

"You've lost me."

"Francisco de Montejo was part of a group of conquistadors who came to the east coast of Yucatán the year after Córdova discovered it in 1517. Whenever they landed for explorations and supplies, the Maya gave them gifts—gold bars, figurines of men with half masks made of gold, crowns of golden beads."

"That's where the poor bastards made their big mistake."

"Of course," Davina agreed. "Still, to the Maya, gold was not as valuable as jade. They associated jade's *yax*—its blue-green color—with the center of the earth. It was also the color of the Tree of Life, water, new corn and all things precious. However, despite their preference for jade, gold certainly wasn't invaluable. They considered it a gift from the sun."

"While to the Spaniards it meant instant prestige, wealth and fame—not to mention a nice little title back home," Sam remarked.

Lines furrowed her smooth brow as she frowned. Sam resisted the impulse to rub them away with his finger. "That's right," she replied and exhaled a soft, regretful sigh at the idea of the conquistadors' ill-gotten gains. "Anyway, Montejo invited Guerrero to join the Spanish conquerors, but not only did he steadfastly refuse, he later led the Mayan warriors against the Spanish."

"That must have pleased the conquistadors no end," Sam said as he stubbed out his cigarette.

He admittedly didn't have Davina's vast knowledge of Mayan culture, but Sam was familiar with the methods the

Spanish had utilized in conquering the Western hemisphere. However brutal the Maya had recently been proved to be, the conquistadors were certainly no slouches when it came to warfare and torture.

"Actually, Guerrero was considered quite an admirable adversary," she said thoughtfully. "The Spaniards respected bravery and several actually attributed their own military reverses to Guerrero's genius. Unfortunately, he was outnumbered when he took a handpicked force of troops to Honduras by canoe to assist the Indians there in their fight against the invading armies. After leading his contingent against Pedro de Alvarado's soldiers, Guerrero was found dead on the field, dressed and painted and ceremonially lacerated. He died as he had lived," she finished softly. "Bravely."

Sam stared at the sudden pain in her eyes. He had the uneasy feeling that Davina was actually envisioning the scene of the brutal battle. "You really take this stuff seriously, don't you?"

She managed a crooked, self-deprecating smile. "Sorry. I tend to get carried away from time to time."

She was reminding him of her father more with each passing moment. Sam found the idea of Jordan Lowell's death even more unpalatable today than when the rumors of the man's demise had begun to circulate last year—because now someone else was involved. And Davina Lowell was a very appealing woman. She was also obviously intelligent. But she was undeniably, damnably vulnerable. Left to her own devices, she'd only end up getting hurt.

Why me? Sam considered bleakly. Even as he asked himself the rhetorical question he knew the answer. He had discovered long ago that there was no place on earth a man could go to escape his destiny. He was responsible, however indirectly, for a grave injustice being done. Obviously, fate had sent Davina Lowell to Calderitas to even the score.

There were no two ways about it; it was clearly up to him to keep her out of trouble. He had owed Jordan Lowell for a long, long time. Perhaps this would finally settle the score and allow him to sleep again, free of the recurring nightmares that no amount of tequila had been able to banish entirely.

As a significant silence swirled about them, Davina felt more than a little foolish to have been caught being so emotional about an event that had happened more than 470 years ago. She wrapped up her story in a brisk no-nonsense tone.

"After the battle, some of his followers, along with his wife and two sons, disappeared."

Like Jordan Lowell. Sam refrained from sharing with Davina the more graphic of his ideas about her father's probable fate.

"A lot can happen in the jungle," he commented carefully. "If the boa constrictors or coral snakes don't get you, there's always the jaguars. Not to mention outlaws, pumas, malaria—"

"I get your drift, Mr. McGee," Davina said calmly. "How strange that my sources didn't bother to mention your fear of the unknown." Davina knew she'd gone too far when a storm suddenly clouded his eyes.

"There's a world of difference between fear and common sense," he pointed out quietly.

Dangerous golden eyes dueled with vivid turquoise ones for an immeasurable time. Davina was the first to lower her gaze. "Do you want to hear the rest of this story or not?" she asked quietly, idly tracing with her fingernail the initials carved into the wooden tabletop by previous customers of the cantina.

Sam leaned back in his chair, striking a match on the heel of his boot as he lit yet another cigarette. "By all means carry on," he invited in a deep drawl. "I have a feeling that you're just getting to the good part."

Davina glared at him through the smoke. "You realize, of course, that those things will kill you."

His lips quirked. "Worried about me, Davina?"

"Of course not," she retorted, unnerved by the sudden light in his eyes.

Sam rubbed his chin thoughtfully. "Let me guess the ending to this intriguing little tale....You're about to tell me that Guerrero's followers built a vast city, named it Naj Taxim and continued living there in peace and harmony with only occasional excursions into the outside world."

"That's right." Her stern gaze defied argument.

Sam heaved a deep sigh of resignation. "I still think you're crazy as a bedbug, Davina Lowell. But I'm willing to offer you a compromise."

Davina's eyes narrowed suspiciously. From what she had seen of Sam McGee thus far, she would have thought the word *compromise* was not in the man's vocabulary.

"What type of compromise?"

"I'll take you as far as Chichén Itzá," he suggested. "Then, if the guy with the map doesn't show up, you call off this wild-goose chase and go back home to your nice, safe, ivory tower of academia."

Davina wasn't overly pleased with his description of her admittedly unexciting life. It certainly wasn't her fault that the dwindling number of suitable excavations, as well as the constant struggle for funds, left the majority of archaeologists confined to classrooms and museums. Admittedly, with the exception of a summer spent outside Mexico City researching Aztec ruins, that had been Davina's fate.

But all that was going to change once she found her father; faced with her accomplishment, he would have to see that his daughter had indeed grown up while he had been trekking around his various jungles. He would finally realize that she would be a valuable addition to his team. Davina refused to permit herself to fail.

"And if there is a map?" she countered.

Responsibility warred with logic as Sam considered her question. Common sense assured him that there was no map—just as there was no Naj Taxim. Her father was dead. A regretful fact, but a fact just the same. The sooner Davina Lowell faced the truth, the better off she'd be.

But something about her made it difficult to refuse her outright. Perhaps it was the blatant hope shining in those wide aquamarine eyes. Or perhaps it was the fragrance that surrounded her—a crisp, clean scent that reminded him of perpetual springtime. Or, Sam considered with his typical honesty, perhaps it was simply that it had been a very long time since he'd bedded any woman, let alone one from that faraway world he'd left behind. Whatever the reason, he found himself ducking her question.

"Let's take this one step at a time," he said simply. "Beginning with Chichén Itzá. When are you supposed to meet this guy?"

"Friday. Does this mean you'll take the job?"

Damn. The day after tomorrow. That didn't allow much time to run a check on Davina's map salesman. "I don't come cheap," he warned.

"While we Yankees are infamous for haggling over bargains, we also appreciate value, Mr. McGee," Davina said seriously. "I've been assured that you're the best. I expect to pay for quality work."

Sam had to give her credit. When he named an outrageously padded fee, in a last-ditch attempt to send her running back to Boston, Davina paled but nodded bravely.

"I'll call my bank and have them wire a draft for ten days' work." While she struggled to remain composed and not reveal the shock that Sam's alleged fee had been, Davina spoke in a voice not nearly as strong. "Do you think that will give us enough time?" she asked hopefully.

"You never know, Ms Lowell," he responded laconically. "Chasing a legend takes time."

"Time," she repeated flatly, not looking at all encouraged.

He gave her a wicked grin. "That's right. Even on the crazy, outside chance you get your map, landmarks will have changed a great deal over the centuries. The entire trek could take a month or two. Maybe even three, considering the fact that it's the rainy season."

Davina's heart sank to the sawdust-covered floor as she began mentally calculating the man's daily fee times ninety days. She'd be lucky not to have to hock her great-grandmother Lowell's silver service just to get herself through the first month. What on earth was she going to do if the expedition dragged on longer than that? Refusing to consider the matter, Davina held out her hand.

"Mr. McGee, consider yourself hired."

He took the slender hand she offered, surprised to find that Davina possessed a strength not apparent at first glance. Her skin was smooth, her fingernails, free of polish, had been buffed until they gleamed. For a fleeting instant Sam pictured those creamy, slender hands on his body, her fingers trailing tantalizingly over his skin.

Don't be a damned fool, he told himself. *This one is so far out of your league that you don't even belong in the same ballpark, McGee.* Even as Sam warned himself of that fact, he admitted that though Sam McGee, expatriate cantina owner, might not have anything in common with Ms Davina Lowell, Samuel Matthew McGee was another matter altogether.

He shook his head in disgust at himself. He'd put that life behind him and he wasn't going to look back, even if Davina Lowell was the most enticing lure he'd had thrown at him in the past five years. He'd pay off the damn debt to her father as swiftly and uneventfully as he could. Then he'd put the lady on a plane and send her back to Boston where she belonged.

Not for the first time, certainly, Davina told herself that she had to be insane, throwing her lot in with this man. She watched cautiously as his face hardened to granite and his tawny eyes turned to agate.

"Mr. McGee?"

Her soft tone cut through his introspection. Sam's eyes followed hers to their linked hands, and he belatedly realized that his fingers had tightened uncomfortably around hers.

"Sorry," he said gruffly, yanking his hand away.

Davina put her hands in her lap, surreptitiously rubbing them together to stimulate circulation. Her eyes remained wary. "I should probably be getting back to Molly's," she suggested quietly. "It's been a long day."

Sam appeared almost relieved as he jumped to his feet. "Good idea. I'll walk you there."

Davina knew better than to refuse his offer. Besides, as strange a man as Sam McGee was, her instincts told her that she was a great deal safer with him than she'd be taking her chances on her own.

"Thank you," she said formally.

An awkward silence hovered between them as they walked the few short blocks to Molly's place. Once, when she inadvertently brushed against him, Sam recoiled, jamming his hands deep into his pockets as he kept to the very edge of the sidewalk. His total lack of interest left her feeling vaguely disappointed, but Davina reminded herself that the last thing she wanted was to have to fend off passes from a man she'd be working so closely with.

Besides, Sam McGee wasn't even her type. As a rule, she preferred educated, intelligent men; men with ambition and drive. Men like her father; like Brad. The thought of her father's assistant made her sigh with regret. She'd always valued their friendship as something special.

Davina had been much too busy these past years establishing her career to consider the idea of marriage and a family seriously, yet during random moments of introspection she had considered becoming Mrs. Bradford Stevenson someday. The idea of having someone to share her work with outside the corridors of Boston University was undeniably appealing.

Now, after Brad's refusal to accompany her to the Yucatán, she was forced to consider the unpalatable fact that he didn't take her any more seriously than her father had all these years. She could have understood his misgivings; in her more rational moments, even Davina had to admit she was playing a long shot, coming down here to search for a man everyone had written off as dead months ago.

No, she thought sadly, what had hurt her was Brad's stubborn refusal to stand by her. If he had honestly cared about her, wouldn't he at least have tried to understand her need to come to Mexico? If he'd felt something special for her, might he not have wanted to be with her at this time?

Her soft, rippling sigh drew Sam's attention. "Tired?"

"A little," she admitted, rubbing the back of her neck wearily. "Although I don't know why I should be after this afternoon's nap."

"It's the humidity. You'd better get used to it. It'll be a helluva lot worse in the jungle."

"You don't have to worry about me," she countered stiffly. "I'm a lot stronger than I look."

"That's right, you're the lady who breaks bricks with your bare hands, aren't you?" There was no mistaking the acid sarcasm in his voice.

Davina murmured something vague that could have been agreement. Before Sam had a chance to dwell on her non-committal answer, two men came barreling out of a tavern, fists flailing. Taking her arm, he moved her off the sidewalk, into the street, out of the way of the crowd that immediately followed the dueling pugilists.

"I'll say this for you, Mr. McGee," she said conversationally, once they had returned to the wooden sidewalk, "when you decided to run away from home, you certainly chose a colorful place."

Sam's fingers tightened on her arm. "What makes you think I'm running away from anything?" His tone was gruff; his eyes, in the spreading glow of a flashing neon sign, hard and unyielding.

Davina had not put a great deal of thought into her words; indeed, they'd come off the top of her head in an attempt to lighten the silence mounting between them, as thick and uncomfortable as the moisture-laden night air. Now, considering his obvious tension, she found herself suddenly very curious about this guide she had hired. Who was Sam McGee? And what was he doing hiding out in this harbor town on the edge of nowhere?

She forced an uncaring shrug, reminding herself that her sole interest in Sam McGee was as a guide.

"It was simply a casual statement, Mr. McGee," she assured him calmly. "There's no reason to bite my head off."

Sam's narrowed eyes were riveted on her own wide, guileless ones. Try as she might, she couldn't entirely conceal the feminine curiosity lingering in their depths. *Trouble*, he reminded himself. *Davina Lowell is nothing less than a disaster just waiting to happen.*

If he had any sense at all, he'd put her on that damn plane tomorrow and send her back to her nice tidy existence with that professor in Boston, before things got out of control. The problem with that plan was that the lady wouldn't go, he reminded himself, his silent scrutiny taking in the stubborn tilt of her chin.

"Let's just get you back to Molly's before you get into more trouble," he suggested brusquely, putting an end to the conversation.

As they continued walking, Davina came to the reluctant conclusion that Sam's gritty suggestion had come too late; because every feminine instinct she possessed told her that she had already gotten herself into more trouble than she could have imagined.

Despite the fact that her archaeological excursions had previously been limited to Mexico City and its environs, Davina had no qualms about the upcoming expedition; she was confident enough to believe that she could handle any situation that might arise.

But Sam McGee was turning out to be another story altogether: Davina had the uneasy feeling that this man was going to prove far more challenging, notably more dangerous than anything she could possibly come up against in the Yucatán jungle.

HE NEVER SHOULD HAVE AGREED to this wild-goose chase, Sam told himself the next morning as they drove to Chichén Itzá. He should have turned her down flat. So what if she got herself mixed up with one of those other unsavory characters on her damned list? What business was it of his? Who had appointed him Davina Lowell's keeper?

Fate, he reminded himself grimly. Despite every logical argument to the contrary, Sam couldn't discount the fact that the odds of Jordan Lowell's daughter suddenly showing up in Calderitas were slim to nonexistent. That she had beaten those odds simply proved that a man could not outrun his destiny.

Davina gripped the edges of the torn vinyl seat of the Jeep with white-knuckled fingers as Sam seemed determined to hit every single pothole from Calderitas to Chichén Itzá. He hadn't said a word since they had left the immigration checkpoint a few miles outside Chetumal. And even then, he had practically bitten her head off when she had offered to reimburse him for the "document-checking fee."

Davina was not at all surprised when the officials at the immigration station expected remuneration for services that should ordinarily have been part of their job. That was only standard operating procedure in this country; a prudent traveler always carried additional cash for such instances.

Still, she was admittedly puzzled when Sam nearly threw her money back in her face. His sudden concern for her funds was especially perplexing as he had appeared to have no qualms about his outrageous fee. From that point on, his conversational skills seemed to deteriorate to an occasional grunt. Giving up, Davina turned her attention to the scenery, such as it was.

The land was predominantly flat, the grassy savanna with its low, shrubby vegetation giving way to tropical forest. The air was heavy with moisture, so thick and stifling that Davina had the impression she could reach out and grab fistfuls of the stuff.

Despite the fact that she'd dressed comfortably in a camisole top and shorts, by the time they were five miles out of Calderitas, her clothing was clinging damply to her skin. Her hair, in its usual braid down her back, felt like a heavy, wet rope. Dust drifted over the interior of the Jeep. Mingling with the perspiration glistening her skin, it made unattractive streaks down her arms and legs.

She had been tempted to ask Sam to take the turnoff that would have led them to Laguna Bacalar—the Lagoon of the Seven Colors. The idea of plunging into the cooling waters was definitely appealing. But she was forced to acknowledge that any delay—no matter how refreshing—would only prolong the agony. Oh, how she longed to reach Valladolid, where they would be spending the night before continuing on to the Mayan ruins in the morning. Right now, she'd give everything she owned for a bathtub—preferably filled with ice cubes.

"Can't you go any faster?" she asked crankily after they'd been on the road for what seemed like hours. She had been studying the map spread across her thighs and was distressed that they had not made an encouraging amount of progress.

The look Sam gave her appeared to question her sanity. "Sure, if you want to break an axle. In case you've noticed, sweetheart, this road isn't exactly the Massachusetts Turn-pike."

His casual mention of her hometown expressway got her attention instantly. It wasn't much, but she was astute enough to realize that she'd just been handed a clue to his background.

"You've been to Boston."

"A few times," he responded noncommittally.

"So," she mused aloud, "you must have lived on the East Coast."

He couldn't resist a half smile at Davina's less-than-subtle digging. "I grew up in Philadelphia," he was surprised to hear himself telling her. "My wife was originally from Boston; we lived in Manhattan."

"You're married?" If she had found this unwilling attraction to Sam McGee unsettling, Davina was appalled at how the idea of Sam's having a wife proved even more distressing.

Sam's face resumed its usual grim expression. "I was married. Past tense."

"Oh."

Davina's gaze moved over Sam's rugged features, taking in his shaggy hair, dark beard and bronzed skin. His shoulders stretched the seams of the white cotton shirt, and as the perspiration-soaked material clung to the rigid lines of his torso, it revealed muscles that were the obvious result of hard, physical labor—and lots of it.

"I can't picture you in Boston," she murmured truthfully. "Or Philadelphia or Manhattan, either, for that matter."

Instead of appearing offended, Sam surprised Davina by laughing. It was a deep, robust sound that pulled some cord deep within her.

"Neither could I." Lines she had only briefly noticed fanned outward from his eyes, hidden by the dark glasses he wore in deference to the sun's glare. Momentarily beguiled, Davina could only stare in response.

"There's a jug of water in the back," he offered suddenly. "It'll have to do for now; as soon as we get to Felipe Carrillo Puerto, we'll stop for lunch and something cool to drink."

Davina had no idea what had caused Sam's abrupt change in attitude, but she was certainly relieved that his earlier ill humor seemed to have evaporated. Unfastening her seat belt, she climbed onto her knees and reached over the back of the seat to retrieve the water jug. When the Jeep hit yet another bump, she was momentarily jostled, but Sam reached out and steadied her before she could lose her balance.

She told herself that it was probably only her imagination, or a case of impending heatstroke, but her body temperature seemed to leap an additional hundred degrees at his touch.

"Are you okay?" he asked as she managed to turn around and sit down once again.

"Just fine."

Davina realized she was holding her breath as she waited irrationally for some ancient Mayan spirit to strike her down for telling such an outrageous falsehood. In truth, she was still shaken by the extent of arousal Sam McGee was able to instill in her with a single look, a casual touch.

Davina was a scholar; she'd spent her life delving into thick texts, seeking answers. In the same manner that she planned her days—indeed, her life—in minute detail, she preferred neat, tidy solutions to problems. The fact that she could not easily explain away these feelings she was experiencing for Sam McGee was both exciting and frightening at the same time. He was like this country, she decided, eyeing him surreptitiously: remote, dangerous and strangely, inexplicably alluring.

"You're a helluva sight more than fine, Davina Lowell," he said under his breath.

His eyes, shielded by the sunglasses, were unreadable, but the huskiness of his voice told its own story. As his gaze flicked over her, moving from the top of her blond head down to her shell-pink toenails, Davina could feel herself literally melting into the seat.

"Would you like a drink of water?" she asked with feigned calm.

"You know what I want, Davina."

Yes, she knew. She had lain awake most of last night thinking of nothing else. Every self-protective instinct had warned her against this man. Even now Davina knew that a wise woman would have thanked the man politely when he had shown up at Molly's this morning, paid him for his time and sent him on his way. Although Sam McGee's reputation as a guide was unparalleled, he certainly wasn't the only man in Mexico capable of reading a map. But, Davina admitted with a characteristic lack of self-deception, he was the only one she wanted.

She took a drink of the lukewarm water before answering. "I know," she admitted, offering him the jug.

"Thanks."

His long, deep swallows made his throat muscles ripple in a way that was anything but calming. Davina wondered how she could possibly be feeling desire when she was so damnably hot and uncomfortable.

"So," he said as he wiped his mouth with the back of his hand and positioned the jug between his legs, "what are we going to do about it?"

Davina shook her head, pretending a sudden interest in the stands of mahogany, cedar, sapodilla and palm trees lining the roadway. "I don't know."

He arched a challenging brow. "Don't you?"

Her lips firmed at his tone. She was grateful for his arrogant behavior. It reminded her that despite his rather earthy appeal, this was not a man any woman would want to get involved with. She had no doubt that Sam was quite proficient in the physical aspects of lovemaking, but he lacked the capacity for tenderness and compassion that would give the act meaning.

"Don't tell me you're one of those women who doesn't believe in mixing business with pleasure," he said into the lingering silence.

"I certainly am."

"Really?" The lazy, masculine challenge in his tone only served to irritate her further.

"Perhaps you're in the habit of falling into bed with every woman who makes the mistake of wandering into that seedy cantina, Mr. McGee, but I'm very particular about the men I make love with."

Sam had to fight the urge to smile when she pulled out that stiff, no-nonsense schoolmarm tone. He wondered if she realized what a challenge she offered when she got up on her high Bostonian horse. What man wouldn't want to be the one to strip away that veneer of cool composure to discover the uninhibited woman he suspected dwelt within?

Of course, there was always the chance that Davina was as crisp, and as no-nonsense a person as she was struggling at this moment to appear. No, Sam decided, her trip down here disproved that theory. Whether she would admit it or not, the lady was a dreamer.

But women who were dreamers alone had no appeal for him; a mere dreamer would have stayed at home in Massachusetts, poring over her ancient text, envisioning what it would be like to search for a fabled city of gold. What he found himself drawn to was Davina's adventurous heart.

Despite the fact that he knew this entire expedition was nothing but sheer folly, Sam had spent much of the past night pondering the outside chance that she might actually have stumbled on to something. It was more than the chance for fame and fortune that had captured his unwilling imagination; it was the quest. How long had it been since he'd been excited about something? Too long, he decided.

Not wanting to dwell on the reasons for that, he returned the conversation to its initial track. "Have there been that many men in your life?" he asked, irritated to discover that he didn't like the idea of other men having shared her bed—her life.

She stiffened. "Really, Mr. McGee, my personal life is—"

"None of my business," he finished blandly.

Davina nodded her blond head. "Exactly."

"So what about the illustrious Professor Stevenson?"

"What about Brad?"

"Is your relationship with Brad merely professional?" He slanted her a long, considering look. "You know, he really isn't the right man for you, Davina."

His lazily drawled statement dripped with self-assurance. Furious, Davina fought the perverse urge to jump out of the moving Jeep and walk back to Calderitas.

"You've been hired to lead me to Naj Taxim, Mr. McGee, nothing more. Nowhere in your job description does it mention offering opinions concerning my love life." She met his maddeningly calm gaze with a furious glare. "Besides, you couldn't begin to understand anything about my relationship with Brad," she tacked on hotly.

Realizing that his eyes had drifted from her face to her breasts, which rose and fell with every deep breath she took in an attempt to calm herself, Davina folded her arms over her chest.

Sam swerved to avoid hitting a lizard—a considerate action that took Davina by surprise. Just when she was wondering if he might not actually be as hard-hearted as he seemed, he returned his gaze to her flushed face.

"I know that self-proclaimed expert on Toltec fetishes doesn't satisfy you."

"Not only are you disgusting," she spat back, "you're dead wrong. Bradford Stevenson satisfies me perfectly in every way; he's everything I could possibly ever wish for in a man."

"Is that so?" he inquired blandly. "Then how do you explain the fact that you spent most of last night wondering how it would be when the two of us made love?"

Sam wondered when he had ever seen anything as lovely as the soft rose color that drifted into Davina's cheeks. When had he last been with a woman capable of blushing?

Her turquoise eyes broke free of his to stare out at the scenery. "I don't know what you're talking about."

He quirked a challenging brow. "Don't you?"

Davina shook her head emphatically. "No." When the word quavered, she repeated it with more vigor. "No."

"If we're going to be working together," he murmured enticingly, "the least we can do is agree not to lie to each other, Davina. There could well be times in the next few days, or weeks, when our lives might depend on knowing we can trust each other."

Trust Sam McGee? The man must think she had a screw loose.

Biting down his frustration at her refusal to answer, Sam pulled the Jeep over to the shoulder. Cutting the engine, he took a cigarette from his shirt pocket and lit it.

"The jungle has enough secrets of its own," he said slowly, keeping his eyes on hers. "Let's not add to the ones we already have going against us."

Damn him. Obviously he realized that her resistance to that deep, velvet voice was very low. Davina's face was set in firm, argumentative lines, but her soft eyes gave her away.

"I don't know what you're talking about," she lied weakly.

"Lovely," he murmured, half to himself.

When she arched an inquiring brow, he gave her a slow, seductive smile. "Your eyes," he explained. "They remind me of the sea. Serene and inviting one moment; then, without warning, they turn dark and stormy. I've come to the conclusion that the turbulence is even more inviting—more exciting."

A strange, alien warmth began to stir deep inside him, but Sam forced it down for the time being. "I spent a great deal of time last night wondering how your eyes are going to look when we make love," he said solemnly.

Unable to resist touching her, he reached out and trailed a finger down her cheek. "They'll appear a great deal like they do at this moment, I think: wide, slightly vulnerable, but laced with a tumultuous passion that's crying out to be released."

Her heartbeat, as it thudded out of control, could have belonged to someone else. "How much tequila have you had to drink today?"

"Not a drop."

Derision flashed in her eyes, replacing the unwilling desire. "Oh, really? Why do I find that extremely difficult to believe?"

A faint but unmistakable irritation flickered in his eyes. He drew in on the cigarette. "Yesterday was—" he paused, as if to choose the correct word, "—difficult. You picked a bad day to arrive in Calderitas."

"From what I've seen thus far, I strongly doubt that Calderitas has many good days."

The desire that had risen to thicken the already steamy air between them slowly evaporated like morning mist under a blazing sun. Sam stubbed out the cigarette in the ashtray, discovering belatedly that he didn't really want it after all.

"It all depends on how you look at things," he said at length. "What you want out of life."

Briefly, for this single isolated moment, Davina forgot both the animosity she had felt for this man from the beginning, and the unwelcome jolts of desire that had occurred with uncomfortable frequency. Instead, she found herself wondering once again what had possessed a man like Sam McGee to turn his back on the world in order to eke out a miserable living as the owner of a decidedly tacky cantina at the very edge of civilization.

"What do you want out of life, Sam?" she asked quietly.

Damn her. Ever since her untimely arrival yesterday, Sam had spent too many hours reviewing his life—in particular that past five years—in minute detail. Davina Lowell reminded him of things he'd left behind; people he had turned his back on; life that, for all it had to do with who he was now, could have belonged to some other man—in another world, in another time.

On the best days, Sam refused to give in to lengthy periods of introspection, finding them nothing but a waste of time and mental energy. To be forced to dwell on such matters on a day when his head felt as if it were stuck in a vise only irritated him more. He was in no mood to be charitable.

For a fleeting instant, his eyes had been unguarded, and Davina thought she could detect a flicker of pain in their amber depths. Before she could be certain, however, he had slid that now familiar scowl over his features.

"Right now," he muttered, "I just want to get this wild-goose chase over with." Throwing back his head, he took another long drink of water before placing the jug on the seat between his legs.

As they continued down the deserted highway, Davina found her eyes continually drawn to the way the hair on his taut thighs gleamed like black gold. When he muttered a low curse and shifted abruptly into second gear, swerving to avoid hitting a particularly deep pothole, she stared, entranced by the play of muscles as he slammed down on the clutch.

"Thirsty?"

As his voice broke into her consciousness, Davina dragged her gaze guiltily to his face, not surprised to see a bold, knowing expression on his dark features. He had been well aware of her feminine scrutiny and couldn't resist the chance to let her know.

"Not particularly. Thank you, anyway, though." Her tone was crisp, her eyes averted, as she returned her attention to the map.

Sam glared down in frustration at the glossy blond head. "The hell with it," he ground out. A moment later, he pulled the Jeep once again to the side of the highway, cut the ignition and tossed the water jug into the back of the Jeep.

Davina glanced up from her pretended scrutiny of the road map. "What do you think you're doing now?"

"What I should have done the minute you walked into the cantina."

His fingers dispensed with Davina's seat belt before she could utter a single word of protest. A moment later, he pulled her into his arms.

Davina reeled from the raw hunger of Sam's lips as he crushed his mouth to hers. Despite the fact that she hadn't been able to help fantasizing about this kiss during the unreasonably lonely hours the previous night, she could not have imagined the tempest that suddenly swirled around her and Sam in the moist, heavy air. Passion scorched away protest, need dissolved reason, as they were caught in a storm neither of them could control.

Sam was not gentle, but Davina didn't want gentleness. There was an aggressiveness in the kiss, a harshness that might have frightened her had her own needs not been equally as powerful, as urgent. Her lips clung to his, avidly, hungrily; her hands fretted over his back in a desperate need to touch, to feel. When his hands cupped her breasts, Davina arched against him, inviting increased intimacies; when his fingers trailed up the warm flesh of her thighs, a soft moan escaped her throat.

Needs—hot and unrestrained—surged through Sam's body until he thought he'd explode. Just as he had not rationally planned this kiss, neither could he have predicted Davina's forthright response. He struggled for some slender thread of sanity, telling himself that if he didn't call a halt to this now, he'd end up taking her in the back of the Jeep. Not that it would be the first time Sam had resorted to such tactics, but something told him that this woman was different.

Colors were swirling in Davina's head—brilliant, glorious colors that echoed the flaming warmth surging through her body. Crimson, gold, amethyst—dazzling hues that tilted and shifted like facets of a child's kaleidoscope. When Sam suddenly pulled his head back, breaking the heated contact, she nearly cried out in dismay.

"Sam?" She blinked slowly as she stared up at the granite face.

Her turquoise eyes, darkened with unmistakable desire, reminded him of a storm-tossed sea and made Sam doubt his sanity. There he was, on the brink of making love to a passionate, willing woman, and he was backing away from what he sensed could be an unequaled experience. What in the hell had Davina Lowell done to his mind?

"I thought you were in such a god-awful hurry to get to Valladolid." His chest rose and fell as he fought to catch his breath.

Davina could feel the jackhammer beat of his heart under her fingertips and realized that he had an amazing amount of self-control to stop while his body was still encouraging fulfillment. She knew that if she wanted to emerge from this with a vestige of self-esteem she would have to display the same restraint.

"I was." Despite her whirling head, her tone was matter-of-fact.

Sam plunked her unceremoniously back onto her own seat. "Then we'd better get this show on the road." His fingers, as they twisted the key in the ignition, were not as steady as he would have liked.

But he need not have worried; with her curious gaze directed at his shuttered features, Davina failed to notice. "I suppose so," she murmured distractedly. When he didn't respond, she turned her attention to the road.

Davina had no idea how long they remained that way, eyes directed straight ahead as they continued down the highway, not exchanging a word, but it seemed like hours.

Finally, when she couldn't stand the stifling silence any longer, she risked a look in his direction.

"Sam?"

"What?" He kept his gaze directed out the windshield, not trusting himself to remain unmoved by the soft vulnerability he knew he'd see on her face.

"I don't understand," she said quietly.

Biting back a low oath, Sam wondered how a woman with Davina's penchant for recklessness had managed to survive this long. So far, in the past twenty-four hours, she'd entrusted her luggage to one of Calderita's more infamous crooks, wandered unescorted into a waterfront cantina and announced her crazy plan to traipse across miles of jungle, seeking a damned city everyone knew was only legend, and a man who'd been declared dead more than a year ago.

In addition to all that, she didn't even have enough sense to tell him to go to hell after he'd practically raped her out on a deserted stretch of Yucatán highway. Like a moth flitting around a flame, Davina Lowell was playing with fire. The damnable thing about all this was that it was up to him to keep her from getting burned.

"For an educated woman, you sure can act like a dumb female," he pronounced.

Eyeing his grimly set mouth, Davina had the strange feeling that Sam was every bit as angry with himself as he was with her—perhaps even more so.

"Please don't be sorry," she said. "I'm not."

His answering look could have cut diamonds. Davina decided not to press her luck. She turned her head, pretending an avid interest in the scenery.

By the time they had reached Felipe Carrillo Puerto, Sam's bad humor seemed to have mellowed. His mood, though certainly not expansive, was no longer threatening, and his eyes had lost their brittle hardness.

The town, at the junction of three major highways, had developed into a pleasant commercial center. During lunch at a sidewalk café, Sam told her that it was a base for *chicleros*, the men who gathered the sap of the nearby *chico zapote* tree for use as the base of chewing gum.

Originally known as Chan Santa Cruz, the town had come into existence in the 1850s, when a rebel group of Maya settled in the area. Like the ancient Mayan cities, Chan Santa Cruz was a holy place, a ceremonial center where only a few of the leaders and priests were permitted to live. Davina remembered having read that the town had been the capital of the independent Mayan territory for almost half a century.

She pressed the soda bottle against her forehead, willing the icy condensation to work miracles and cool her overheated body.

"I thought this was supposed to be the rainy season."

"It is."

She cast a hopeful glance upward. "Then why doesn't it rain?"

Sam had to admit a grudging admiration for her; she hadn't offered a word of complaint all morning, when it was obvious that the enervating heat and humidity were causing her a great amount of distress. Of course, she had managed to start a little fire herself with that surprising response to his kiss.

He tipped the bottle of water he'd ordered for her, wetting a paper napkin. "Rain would only make it worse," he said as he reached across the small table and wiped her brow. "All it does is raise the humidity; the heat doesn't go away."

"That feels nice," she murmured, closing her eyes as he moved the damp napkin over her face.

Her cheeks were brightly pink, unnatural against the creamy complexion of the rest of her skin. She wasn't meant for a life in the jungle. Davina Lowell belonged in a drawing room in some Beacon Hill town house, pouring tea from an heirloom silver service crafted by Paul Revere. He could easily envision her surrounded with dark, gleaming wood, Oriental rugs and bookcases filled with leather-bound first editions. Sam decided to give her one last chance to change her mind.

"You can always call this off. No one could accuse you of not trying, Davina."

She opened her eyes, and Sam could not help but recognize the determination he viewed in those solemn turquoise depths. She had her father's eyes, he realized—as well as her father's ambition and academic bent. But there the similarity ended.

Her father would never have been capable of those flashes of fiery passion he had witnessed in Davina. The only thing Sam had ever known Jordan Lowell to get excited about was his work. It said something about the archaeologist's single-mindedness that despite the years he had known Jordan, despite the months they had worked together, the man had only casually mentioned a daughter. And never had he revealed that she was so attractive.

"I'm not going back, Sam. Not until I find Naj Taxim. And my father."

He dropped the napkin onto the red-and-white checkered oilcloth covering the wooden table. "Are all the Lowells this damn stubborn?" It was a rhetorical question; he knew the answer all too well.

"So I've been told."

Sam leaned back in the chair as he tipped the bottle of beer to his lips, eyeing her reflectively. After a long, thoughtful pause, he looked down at his watch. "Since you refuse to listen to reason, I suppose we should get going."

Davina cast one last wistful glance at the creaky paddle-blade fan, which had been putting up a valiant attempt to circulate the moist air. The slight breeze had been most welcome.

"I suppose so," she said agreeably, not wanting to admit that the idea of going back out onto that blistering high-way was the last thing she wanted to do.

They were approximately five miles out of town when Davina could not keep her thoughts to herself any longer.

"Sam?"

He had barely heard her soft, hesitant tone over the drone of the motor. "Yeah?"

"About earlier—"

He brought his hand down viciously, forestalling her next words. "Forget it."

He knew what she was going to bring up and he damn well didn't want to discuss the subject. Sam didn't know which he regretted more—initiating that damned kiss or failing to follow through on it.

"I don't think I can," she said truthfully. Even now, she could feel the pressure of his lips on hers, the strength of his hands roving her body. Davina did not want to leave the is-sue unresolved.

The look he gave her was cold, hard. "Try."

5

FIFTEEN MILES from Valladolid, the wind suddenly picked up. Pulling over to the side of the road, Sam put the top up on the Jeep as slate-black clouds rolled ominously across the sky, blocking out the sun. Moments later, the darkened sky opened up and the driving rain came down in torrents.

More accustomed to the gentle afternoon rains of Mexico City, Davina was somewhat frightened by the harshness of the storm. But she kept silent, allowing Sam to concentrate on maneuvering the car through the flowing washes. By the time they entered Valladolid, the second-largest town in Yucatán, she was exhausted. She was even too tired to offer the slightest murmur of resistance when Sam drove directly to a hotel in the center of town and, while she sank wearily onto a rattan chair in the lobby, registered them into adjoining rooms.

"I suppose it would be asking too much to hope my room has a bathtub," she said as they rode the elevator to the second floor of the hotel. The ancient cage creaked ominously as if complaining about the weight.

He smiled a little. "Not only do your accomodations have a bathtub, but the clerk on duty assured me that your room also boasts air-conditioning. It's one of the few in this place that does."

The idea of lounging in a tub of tepid water while the cool breeze from the air-conditioning duct blew over her made Davina want to fling her arms around Sam's neck in heartfelt gratitude. Instead, she gave him a wide smile.

"Sam McGee, I do believe you're a miracle worker!"

Davina looked as if she'd just gotten the deed to her very own diamond mine. Sam was surprised to find that she could be excited by such a simple thing; still, as unaccustomed to the heat as she obviously was, air-conditioning had to be a decided plus.

"Air conditioning." Davina sighed happily. "I owe you one, McGee."

Sam looked at her for a long moment. Just when Davina thought he was going to actually break down and say something personal, perhaps even profound, the elevator reached their floor and the wrought-iron cage door opened.

"You don't owe me a thing," he responded with a careless shrug. "Don't forget, you're paying for this place."

His biting tone caused her newfound temper to rise. Why on earth had she expected any display of human warmth from this man? Fatigue, as well as discomfort from a day on the road in temperatures resembling a sauna, conspired to make her words rash. "How could I possibly forget?" she snapped. "With you around to remind me."

Sam appeared unperturbed by Davina's sarcasm as he unlocked the door to her room. "Perhaps I'm simply reminding myself," he said quietly as he placed her suitcase on the bed. Before his words had a chance to sink in, he had dropped her key on the top of the mahogany dresser and left the room.

Sinking onto the too-soft mattress, Davina stared at the door he'd closed behind him. If she lived to be a hundred years old, she'd never understand Sam McGee.

Later, as she soaked in an ancient, claw-footed bathtub, the water up to her chin, Davina asked herself why she even wanted to understand the man. He was ill-tempered, uncouth and unpleasant. He could no more understand how to treat a lady than she could fit into the rough-and-tumble life-style he obviously relished in Calderitas.

That was another thing, she considered, doing her best to chalk up reasons that she wanted nothing to do with her bad-tempered guide. If the man had one ounce of gumption, he wouldn't be hiding away from the world, content to sit around and drink tequila in that horrid cantina.

"It doesn't make any sense," she murmured, running the bath sponge over her arms. "If he's honestly so terrible, so unattractive, why can't I stop thinking about him this way?"

Because, an impish little voice in the back of her mind piped up, *in spite of all his shortcomings, Sam McGee is one terrific kisser.*

"That's ridiculous," Davina answered aloud. "I'm thirty years old, for heaven's sake. Grown women do not get all soppy over a man just because of a single kiss."

But, oh, what a kiss! the rebellious little voice pointed out accurately—much too accurately for Davina's comfort. She could feel the heat infiltrating her body even now.

She wasn't really sorry about the feelings he'd evoked. After all, he was a strong, physically compelling male. And she was a normal woman, with a normal woman's needs and desires. Add to that the fact that they were partners in what could only be considered a highly romantic, admittedly dangerous adventure, and it was only natural that she should find herself attracted to him.

When she looked at it that way—logically, scientifically—Davina felt immeasurably better. After all, such feelings of passion were to be expected under these conditions. She was only regretful that they were directed toward the worst possible candidate.

Exhaling a soft sigh, Davina leaned her head back against the tin-lined bathtub and closed her eyes. A moment later she had fallen asleep.

In the stifling heat of the unair-conditioned room next door, Sam paced the floor, damning himself for allowing a woman—and a skinny one at that—to get under his skin this way. Despite the fact that emotional involvement with Davina Lowell was the last thing he wanted, he couldn't keep himself from worrying about her—caring about her health, her happiness, her future.

He didn't want to care about anyone. That was what this self-imposed exile had been all about. Five years ago Sam McGee had deliberately, irreversibly, turned his back on responsibility. He'd shucked his custom-tailored suits, the Manhattan penthouse and the Lear jet without a backward glance. And Melanie.

A frown darkened his face as he thought back on his beautiful blond wife. Until this moment, Sam had not realized exactly how much Davina reminded him of her. Not in appearance—he couldn't imagine Melanie covered with a layer of Yucatán dust, her skin glistening with beads of perspiration. During the three years of their ill-fated marriage, he had never witnessed a platinum hair out of place. Her makeup had always been perfect, her clothing both immaculate and one of a kind.

In that respect, Melanie Kirkland had always reminded him of one of those damned pieces of porcelain she was always buying. Expensive, smooth and cold. Again, nothing like Davina, he was forced to admit; Davina had a potential for heat and passion that was overwhelming in its enormity. As his body began to glow with a white-hot flame at the memory of that fiery kiss, Sam lit a cigarette and forced his mind back to the comparison between Davina and his ex-wife.

It was their similar backgrounds, he decided as he drew on the cigarette, feeling the acrid, but strangely comforting smoke filling his lungs. Both women had been born into wealth and privilege. Both had strong, unrelenting fathers—fathers they adored; men whom they would always put before any others. Sam didn't regret the failure of his marriage. What did irk, however, was the fact that Melanie had never understood one thing about him: his feelings; his overwhelming sense of guilt over what had happened. She had, as expected, sided with her father, turning her back on a marriage that should have been declared legally dead at the altar.

Actually, the only thing about those days Sam found himself missing periodically was the hand-built Aston Martin with its four-wheel independent suspension, rack-and-pinion steering and twenty-three coats of lacquer that made looking into its finish like falling into a pool. Although he had never actually attempted the feat, there was something undeniably exciting about being behind the wheel of a car capable of going one-fifth the speed of sound.

Power was always exhilarating, and he had certainly attained his share of that over the years. But everything had its price, and Sam had learned the hard way that the higher the rewards, the greater the ultimate cost.

Unwilling to dwell on something that he could not change, Sam returned his mind to Jordan Lowell's daughter, who at this very moment was probably lounging in the bathtub, hidden by an enticing layer of bubbles. Lord, how he'd love to join her! Opting for the next best thing, Sam picked up the telephone and dialed Davina's room.

The shrill ring of the telephone eventually filtered its way into Davina's consciousness, jerking her out of her sleep just before she slid under the water. Grabbing a towel and wrapping it hastily around her body, she raced into the adjoining bedroom.

"Yes?"

"It took you long enough to answer the phone." Sam hadn't meant to complain. How could he explain that when she didn't answer on the first ring, he had been afraid she'd decided to go off to Chichén Itzá herself?

Davina struggled to ignore the rush of sheer pleasure Sam's deep voice instilled. His irritated tone should have irked her; instead she was melting like honey under the hot sun.

"I was asleep."

"Oh." Damn, he should have thought of that. Where was his mind these past two days? "I'm sorry I woke you."

She noted the apology without commenting on it. Davina knew that words of contrition would not come easily for this man. She took the fact that he'd made the effort as an encouraging sign.

"It's just as well you did," she answered, allowing the smile to creep into her voice. "I was about to go under; you probably saved me from becoming yet another one of those dreary statistics on bathroom safety."

"Dammit," he snarled, "you could have drowned."

"I doubt that," Davina responded calmly. "If you got me out of the bathtub just to yell at me, Sam, I think I'll hang up now; I'm dripping all over the floor."

At the thought of Davina's nude body, only a few feet away, with nothing but a thin door—albeit a locked one—between them, Sam's blood began to boil.

"I called to invite you to dinner." He managed an offhand tone.

"I'd like that," she replied instantly. "What time?"

"How about an hour?"

"Could we make that thirty minutes instead? I just realized that I'm starving."

Sam wasn't surprised; she'd only picked at her lunch. "Thirty minutes it is."

He could hear the smile blossom in her voice. "Terrific. I'll be ready."

Personally, Sam considered that an overly optimistic promise. He'd never known a woman who could go from tub to dinner engagement in thirty minutes. Melanie had always taken a minimum of two hours to get ready, and she had had a host of individuals to assist. On more than one occasion, when looking over the stack of bills at the end of the month, Sam had complained that he should be allowed to claim her hairdresser, manicurist and dress designer as dependents on his income tax. Melanie had never found the statement the least bit amusing.

Shaking his head at the way his mind insisted on rehashing the past, Sam ran the water for his own bath. He scraped the rough cloth viciously over his body, as if he were hoping not only to scrub away memories of his former wife, but his unwilling desire for Davina Lowell, as well.

IT TOOK A HERCULEAN EFFORT, but Sam managed to keep his erotic thoughts safely banked during dinner. Later, as he sat alone on the balcony outside his room, he was forced to admit that his display of self-control wasn't entirely his own doing. Davina's unfortunate choice of conversational topic had the same effect on his libido as a bucket of ice water, temporarily quelling any thoughts of bedding her that he might have been entertaining.

The waiter had taken their empty plates away and as they lingered over cups of spicy *café de olla*, Davina had begun speaking of her father and how much Jordan Lowell's work had always meant to him.

"It was all he cared about," she said.

"But he had a wife. And a daughter," Sam pointed out, lighting a cigarette. For a moment Davina looked inclined to comment on his action. Apparently changing her mind, she began absentmindedly tracing circles on the white tablecloth with her fingernail.

"I don't remember my mother; she died of a tropical fever she contracted on an expedition with my father when I was very young. As for his daughter..." Her voice trailed off.

Davina was grateful when Sam remained silent, giving her time to work the words past the lump in her throat. "I really should get used to the idea that my father's work will always come first," she murmured. "I understand his dedication. And I admire it, really I do. Still..."

Sam knew Davina was fighting back tears and admired her valiant effort. "You were telling me about his work," he reminded her.

Davina gave him a grateful look before continuing, silently acknowledging his returning the conversation to its initial track. "It really was an all-consuming passion."

She propped her elbows on the table, resting her chin on her linked fingers. "*Is* an all-consuming passion," she corrected swiftly, realizing that she'd been referring to her father in the past tense.

He was alive, Davina assured herself fervently. There were too many things left unfinished between them, too many words left unsaid.

"Davina—" Acting on impulse, Sam ran the back of his hand down her cheek. She went very still.

"No," she whispered. She pressed her fingers against his lips. "Don't say it. Don't you see, Sam, I have to believe he's alive. I can't allow any doubts."

It was impossible to remain unaffected by the desperation in her eyes. Sam wished that he could give her some hope—no matter how slight—some reason to keep believing. But he couldn't. Not without lying to her. And for some strange reason he didn't want any more lies between them.

There was already the one. Unspoken, perhaps, but a lie just the same.

"It means that much to you," he said instead.

Davina let out the breath she had been unaware of holding. "Everything."

"Jordan Lowell is a very lucky man." He laced his fingers through hers. "Not many men can claim such love. Or loyalty."

Davina didn't know which was affecting her more—the warmth in his tawny eyes or the tantalizing touch of his thumb against her palm. Her mouth went suddenly dry.

"The Lowells are big on loyalty."

"So I see."

Her pulse jumped as he pressed his lips against the inside of her wrist. Davina struggled to think of something, anything, to say. "I suppose that's one of the reasons that he was so upset about that horrible trouble in the Amazon basin," she managed weakly.

Admittedly Sam had not been paying a great deal of attention to the conversation, preferring instead to observe how the speeded-up beat of Davina's pulse under his lips was in perfect rhythm with the pounding of his own heart. But as her softly spoken words filtered into his consciousness, his blood chilled to ice.

"What trouble?" he asked, knowing the answer and dreading it.

Confusion came and went in her eyes as she tried to understand what had just happened. The old Sam McGee was back—harsh, aloof, his eyes as hard as agate.

"Really, you can't possibly be interested in all this," she protested, looking up at the clock on the wall. A check of her watch showed it to be running thirty minutes late. "Besides, it's getting late; I thought you wanted to get an early start to Chichén Itzá."

"We've got plenty of time." He raised a finger, ordering another drink.

When he looked questioningly toward Davina, she shook her head, silently declining his unspoken offer. Something told her that she would need all her wits about her for the next few minutes. Although he hadn't raised his voice, Davina knew that his quiet request for her to remain with him was nothing less than an order.

Wondering why Sam was suddenly so interested in her father, when he obviously didn't believe him to still be alive, Davina continued her story.

"My father has always been fascinated with lost cultures. He'd been interested in a tribe rumored to live in a remote region of the Amazon basin and had tried to get funding for an expedition for years, but the archaeological community was convinced the existence of the tribe was nothing but fantasy."

"But it wasn't." His tone was rough, gritty.

Davina looked at Sam cautiously as he tossed down the tequila and immediately returned the glass to the waiter for a refill. "No," she agreed quietly. "It wasn't. The tribe really existed, Sam." A sudden shadow moved over his eyes. "At least it did."

He felt a fist twisting his gut. "But not anymore."

"No. Not anymore." She lowered her eyes to the tablecloth. "Well, to be entirely honest, there are a few scattered members left, but in order to survive, they've had to assimilate into other tribes. So even the ones who managed to live lost their entire culture."

When she met his studiously bland gaze, her eyes blazed with anger. "He killed them, Sam. As sure as he took a gun to the heads of every man, woman and child in the tribe and pulled the trigger."

Sam inhaled deeply on his cigarette before commenting on Davina's heated accusation. "You're not talking about your father any longer, are you?" he asked fatalistically.

"Of course not," she retorted. "I'm talking about Palmer Kirkland. He's the one who funded the expedition. And he's the one who single-handedly destroyed an entire civilization."

Not single-handedly, Sam corrected silently, crushing out the cigarette with undue force. "You're right," he said suddenly, pushing away from the table. "It's late. We'd better call it a night."

Davina stared up at him as he stood over her, wondering what it would take to begin to understand the man. She'd never known anyone to run so hot then so icy cold all in the span of a few swift seconds. How she'd love to know what was going on behind those hard, amber eyes.

When he met her questioning stare with a shuttered, inscrutable gaze, Davina reminded herself that she didn't give a damn about Sam McGee's quicksilver moods—just as she didn't care one iota about the man himself. But since she did care about her father, she'd have to put up with this man until he managed to take her to Naj Taxim, where, as far as she was concerned, he could fling himself off the nearest pyramid.

"That's a splendid idea." She rose from the table and walked regally out of the dining room.

Tossing a few colorful bills onto the table, Sam followed. Perhaps it was only his overactive imagination, stimulated by two drinks in swift succession, but he could have sworn he saw a crown perched atop Davina's blond head.

They didn't speak in the elevator, the heavy silence smothering them in the small wrought-iron cage. When they reached Davina's door, Sam muttered a curt good-night before continuing on to his own room. Although he did not look back, he could not miss the sound of Davina's door slamming shut with a decisive bang.

6

AN HOUR LATER, as he sat out on the balcony, Sam's stomach was still tied up in knots. It was obvious that Davina trusted him; no woman would go trekking off into the jungle with a man she didn't trust. Strike that, he corrected grimly. The woman had already proved herself to be a rotten judge of character; hadn't she blithely handed her luggage over to Manuel? Sam wondered what Davina would say if she knew she'd put her life in the hands of a man who—however indirectly—was responsible for genocide.

A harsh word, he mused, drawing on a cigarette. The bright flare momentarily glowed orange in the darkness. But an accurate one, just the same. In his own defense, he hadn't wanted to go to work for Melanie's father. But the Kirkland Foundation had been in dire need of a manager, and if there was one thing Sam knew how to do, it was to make money.

More than one envious individual in those glory days had accused Sam of selling his soul to the devil in exchange for insider tips on the stock market. Everything he touched inevitably turned to gold, to dividends, to profits. The word on Wall Street was that Samuel Matthew McGee could do no wrong. In an odd sort of way, Sam himself had begun to believe his own press—until that fiasco in the Amazon.

A person would have had to have spent the past twelve years of his life camped out on the dark side of the moon not to have heard of Palmer Kirkland. Most people, if asked, would call him an archaeologist, and although he possessed no actual degree in the science, Kirkland would be the last person in the world to contradict the description. What he was, Sam reflected bitterly, was a talented showman.

Palmer Kirkland was a television star of the highest magnitude. More famous than J.R., richer than Carson, even more revered than Cosby, Kirkland took the armchair explorer on assaults up the icy side of Mount Everest, treks into ancient Indian burial grounds and expeditions into Africa, China and South America. Thanks to the wonder of satellite dishes, the entire world was able to watch, enthralled, as the man opened ancient tombs, searched out sunken treasure ships, traced ancient trade routes.

The problem with such activities was that they required considerable funds—even more than the lucrative television contracts provided. It had been Sam's task to locate the monies needed to keep the cycle going—a task made easier by the fact that success inevitably begat success. For each expedition that attracted public attention, hundreds of thousands of dollars poured into the coffers of the non-profit "scientific" foundation.

Even as he continued to provide the money for the expeditions, Sam viewed his father-in-law's work as more entertainment than science. The first time he accused Palmer of being nothing more than a carnival huckster, the man had surprised him by laughingly agreeing.

"But you have to admit, Sam, my boy, we give them one helluva show for their money."

Part of the success of the Kirkland Foundation was due to the fact that Palmer insisted on hiring noted experts in the various fields. Want to search for buried treasure off the coast of China? The Kirkland Foundation located an expert in Oriental maritime history from Stanford. Interested in ancient fossils of dinosaur eggs? The foundation turned to an expert from the Smithsonian's department of paleontology.

And when Palmer Kirkland heard of Jordan Lowell's conviction regarding a group of people, distantly related to the Txukahamei warriors of the Amazon basin, living a Stone Age existence deep in the jungle, the calculator the man had for a brain envisioned the Nielsen ratings going off the chart.

It had taken a year to organize the expedition. After that came another six months in the jungle, following trail after trail, dead end after dead end. Finally Sam was forced to report that the project was several hundred thousand dollars over budget. It was his recommendation that the crew give up the futile search and return home. Before his message could get to the tenacious explorers, led by Jordan Lowell, the men had gotten lost. In their attempt to find their way back to civilization, they had stumbled across the village of the Peixotos Indians, a group of people so innocent of the outside world that they had never seen metal, did not know of something as basic as cloth.

Vastly removed from their distant cousins, the Txukahamei, these Peixotos were no warriors. Although some might erroneously refer to them as savages, the tribe disproved that description by welcoming the explorers with open arms. They had immediately offered their visitors food and water and tried, with hand signals, to communicate. Contact had been made; the team had been ecstatic.

It was then that the problems had begun, Sam recalled bitterly. A few of the members of the exploration team, Jordan included, had argued the necessity of keeping the existence of the tribe a secret. They had insisted that the Indians were too peaceful, too ingenuous to survive if they were suddenly overrun by the outside world.

Palmer had not hesitated to remind the outspoken group exactly who held the purse strings for this trek into Amazonia. The special would be filmed, on schedule. After reading the reams of paperwork sent back to the States, Sam had come to the conclusion that it was imperative the tribe be left in peace. Later perhaps, after years of careful, controlled contact, they would be prepared to cope with the changes civilization would bring. But not yet.

He had argued heatedly again and again with his father-in-law over the question of the Peixotos. As the bitterness between the two men had raged, the sham of Sam's marriage had finally crumbled. Sam had not been surprised by Melanie's defection; he had always known where his wife's loyalties lay. He'd left the home they had shared for three years without a backward glance. Unfortunately, there had been nothing he could do to forestall Palmer's intention to air the program.

Within weeks, hordes of archaeologists had descended on the village. They were soon followed by scores of wealthy tourists and other curiosity seekers. As predicted, the group began to slowly disintegrate. The outsiders brought with them a myriad of previously unknown commodities, from simple trinkets to manufactured goods—battery-operated televisions, chain saws, and one well-meaning individual had actually given the chief a twelve-speed blender. Such things served to instill a jealousy that had always been absent in the group-oriented society, and a culture that had never known violence suffered two murders in the first six months after the television special aired in prime time.

With their routine disrupted by the presence of so many outsiders, the villagers failed to plant all the sweet potatoes, squash, peanuts and corn they needed and became undernourished. Slowly, insidiously, their children began suffering from malnutrition.

Despite injections of penicillin, continuing contact with the *civilizados* exposed the Indians to illnesses for which they had built up no natural immunity. During the first nine months, a score had died of influenza. Skin diseases broke out among several of the villagers, while others fell victim to respiratory illnesses. Within two years, the small band of peaceful Indians had been nearly wiped out—ravaged by the forces of civilization.

Guilt had lain heavily upon Sam McGee's broad shoulders. It did not help to remind himself that he had argued Lowell's case and failed. Neither did it ease his conscience to know that he had left the Kirkland Foundation the day the television program had run, coincidentally on his thirty-fifth birthday.

The undeniable fact was that by raising the funds for the expedition, he had been an important member of the team. There was no way he could not hold himself culpable for the project's fatal outcome.

Now, smoking his cigarette as he watched indigo clouds scudding over the crescent moon, Sam wondered what Davina would think of him if she knew the truth. As if conjured up by his bleak thoughts, Davina chose that moment to come out onto her adjoining balcony.

"I couldn't get to sleep," she said by way of explanation.

"I can imagine you'd be excited about tomorrow." He could not trust himself to look at her.

"That, too," she murmured in agreement.

A forthright individual by nature, Davina wanted to explain these strange feelings, to admit that it had been thoughts of Sam that had kept her awake. But nothing in his tone or his demeanor encouraged such candor; he kept his gaze directed out over the sleeping town.

They shared the night for a time. As the soft scent of Davina's perfume drifted on the warm night air, it mingled enticingly with the fragrance of tropical flowers from the courtyard below. Sam tried to remember when he'd wanted a woman more than he wanted Davina at this moment and came up blank.

Davina cast a surreptitious glance his way, sensing a hunger that equaled her own. But there was more than that. Although she knew she could probably be considered certifiable for even considering such an outlandish idea, she couldn't help feeling that Sam was as confused as she was.

"It's a lovely night," she said softly. When the conversation drags, talk about the weather. "I feel as if I could reach up and grab a handful of those stars."

"The clouds are coming in again," he said gruffly. "We'll have more rain before morning."

"I like rain," she offered.

Her friendly attempt at conversation went unappreciated and unreturned as Sam continued to stare out into the well of darkness. Davina stood still and silent, her hands on the wrought-iron railing, watching the glow of Sam's cigarette flicker in the blackness like a firefly.

After what seemed an eternity, Sam reluctantly gave in to her silent appeal and turned his head toward her. He sucked in a harsh, painful breath as the power of Davina's soft smile slammed into him. In that frozen instant, Sam found himself wishing that he had met this woman years ago. Before Melanie, before Palmer Kirkland, before Jordan Lowell and his damned Indians.

"Are you always this reckless?" he asked, not taking his eyes from hers. Somewhere in the distance the soulful song of a Spanish guitar mingled with the evocative music of female laughter in the sultry night air. A slow flame began to spread through him. "Or do you just enjoy playing with fire?"

Davina laughed softly and tossed back her hair. She was wearing it loose tonight; soft, shimmering waves tumbled over her shoulders. The golden strands silvered with moonlight gleamed in the darkness like the glow of the Milky Way.

"If you want the unvarnished truth, this trip to the Yucatán was the first reckless thing I've done in my entire life."

He flipped the cigarette down onto the flagstone courtyard. It glowed for a fleeting moment like the flare of fireworks, then went out.

"Just be careful you don't get more than you bargained for," he warned.

Davina was shaken by the thundercloud that moved across his rough-hewn features. At the best of times, Sam McGee was a long way from movie-star handsome. Now, his face darkened with some emotion she could not quite discern, the man was a very imposing force.

"Really, Sam," she protested, "I'm not some hothouse flower that's going to wilt at the very first sign of trouble. I've been on explorations before." She tried a slight smile, hoping to encourage an answering one from those grimly set lips. "And as you can see, I certainly lived to tell about it."

He pushed himself out of his chair. "I'll meet you downstairs in the dining room tomorrow morning at six o'clock. If you're not ready, I'm not promising to wait."

As he turned to leave, Davina suddenly realized that the veiled emotion she had seen on Sam's stormy features was genuine concern. She told herself that she shouldn't take it personally. He was probably only worried about missing the opportunity, if anything should happen to her, to earn more money in a week than his sleazy cantina collected in a year.

Davina told herself that. But for some strange reason, she couldn't quite make herself believe it.

"Sam?"

At her hesitant tone, he stopped, his hand on the doorknob. Steeling himself against the emotion he'd find in those wide eyes, Sam slowly turned around.

"Yeah?"

"Thank you."

Two little words. That's all they were. Certainly nothing so earth-shatteringly special. So why did they make him want to pull her into his arms and never let go? Shaking his head in annoyance, Sam told himself that yesterday's tequila must have killed off more brain cells than usual. The thoughts he'd been experiencing since this woman walked into the cantina yesterday afternoon were not only unsettling, they were impossibly ridiculous.

Sam had never considered himself a stupid man. A reckless one perhaps. And even, as Molly had pointed out on more than one occasion, an admittedly jaded one. But stupid? Never. Not until now, he qualified grimly.

"Get some sleep," he ordered.

As he returned to his room, Davina couldn't resist a slight smile. Sam McGee wasn't nearly as tough as he liked to let on. For some odd reason, she found that thought distinctly encouraging.

THE PREMONITION came upon him gradually, creeping into his consciousness as he tried to sleep. The nagging little fingers of impending misfortune that had taunted him over the past two days escalated during the long, sultry night in Valladolid, keeping sleep annoyingly at bay. Sam wasn't usually one to believe in premonitions, dreams, fortune-tellers or the like, but he couldn't shake off the feeling that danger was lurking out there, somewhere just beyond his reach.

A feeling had settled over him, like the slate-gray anvil-shape clouds that gathered every afternoon, and as he went downstairs to meet Davina, Sam couldn't shake the vague, uneasy feeling that he was walking straight into the eye of the storm.

At her first glimpse of Sam, Davina was shaken by the evidence he gave of a long and sleepless night. The dark circles under his eyes appeared almost black against his dark skin, and the lines bracketing his firm lips were deeper than she'd yet seen them etched into his forbidding, granite face.

"Good morning," she said quietly.

"Morning."

Well, Davina decided, it was obvious Sam was not a morning person. She made an attempt at casual conversation during the meal, but she could have just as easily been talking to a sphinx. After three aborted tries, she fell silent, sipping her coffee as she waited for Sam to finish his *huevos rancheros*. Not being a breakfast eater herself, the sight of the greasy fried eggs drowning in red chili sauce was definitely unappealing, but Davina wasn't foolish enough to offer any complaints.

As if by silent agreement, neither spoke until they reached Chichén Itzá, twenty-six miles west of Valladolid.

Sam was the first to break the heavy silence. "Where are you supposed to meet this guy?"

The archaeological zone extended over an area of some three square miles, most of it concealed under a luxuriant growth of vegetation. Mayan buildings of great beauty crumbled quietly on one side of the roadway; on the other stood the gray architecture of the Toltecs, a warlike people from Mexico who had ruled in Chichén Itzá after the Mayan collapse.

Davina didn't respond immediately. She was staring in awe at the Pyramid of Kukulcán. Excellently restored and exceedingly impressive in its classic simplicity, the square pyramid towered more than eighty feet into the bright blue sky.

Like most pre-Columbian buildings, the pyramid had been erected in strict accordance with astronomical and astrological requirements. The nine terraces symbolized the nine heavens, and the four staircases, rising at an angle of forty-five degrees, stood for the four cardinal points. Each of the staircases had ninety-one steps, making a total of 364. When added to the summit platform, the total came to the number of days in the year. At the top of the immense platform stood the temple.

"It's magnificent," she murmured with a sigh of sheer admiration.

Who were these people, these ancient Maya, that they could have erected such a tribute to their god-king long before the establishment of what was now considered civilization? The abandoned pyramids stood in silent tribute to a people who had come from the depths of a mystery—and had disappeared the same way.

"You won't get an argument from me," Sam agreed. "You didn't answer my question," he reminded her pointedly. "Where are you meeting your map salesman?"

Davina dragged her gaze away from the large stone snake head on the stairway. "At the Sacred Cenote," she murmured absently. "Look, Sam!" she exclaimed, pointing toward the majestic white ruin of the nearby Temple of the Warriors. "Isn't it incredible?"

As he muttered something she took for agreement, Davina's eyes roamed the site, drinking in the excavation. "Do you realize," she said quietly, "that while Europe was wallowing in the Dark Ages, these people practiced an astronomy so precise that their ancient calendar was as accurate as the one we employ today? They plotted the courses of celestial bodies, and their priests predicted both solar and lunar eclipses. Somehow they calculated the path of Venus with an error of only fourteen seconds a year and pioneered the mathematical concept of zero."

She took a long, deep breath. "How I'd love to know their secrets."

Sam wondered if Davina realized how lovely she was, her face alive with enthusiasm. "When you find Naj Taxim, you can ask them," he said dryly.

"You don't have to be so sarcastic; I'm sorry if I got carried away."

Sam surprised them both by squeezing her shoulder in a brief, reassuring gesture. "You're entitled. It is admittedly overwhelming. I've been here more times than I care to count, and each time it's like the first time. I hope I never get so cavalier that I can remain unaffected by such splendor."

Surprised by his depth of understanding, Davina looked up at him. "Do you know, Sam McGee, just when I've convinced myself that you're impossible, you turn around and display a genuine streak of thoughtfulness. Why can't you just remain a rat so I know where I stand?"

A silken strand of hair had escaped her thick braid and Sam looped it casually behind her ear. The heavily tinted lenses of his sunglasses obscured his eyes, but lines crinkled outward from them, suggesting that they were smiling.

"If that's really what you want, I'll try my best to oblige. After all, you are the boss."

Her lips curved up at the corners. She wasn't aware of leaning imperceptibly toward him. "And don't you forget it," she warned lightly.

He trailed a finger down her cheek. "Are you threatening to dock my pay?"

Davina felt as if he had taken a flaming torch to her skin. *It's the sun*, she assured herself. *Only the sun. And this stifling jungle heat.* "I think it's time to check out this Sacred Cenote," she said quietly.

Sam felt her backing away from the light, carefree moment and knew intellectually that Davina was doing the right thing. But, dear Lord, how he wanted her!

Davina didn't protest the touch of Sam's hand on her back as they turned up the processional causeway toward the most famous of Yucatán's wells. The peninsula boasted many such cenotes—sinkholes in the limestone—that provided the Yucatec Maya with virtually their sole source of water.

A sunny tranquillity enfolded the Well of Sacrifice. Swallows and butterflies darted and fluttered above the opaque green water. Small, blind fish from underground streams that fed the cenote wiggled just below the surface—silver flashes that appeared for an instant before disappearing into the jade-colored depths.

Silence. Serenity. Davina stood at the edge of the cenote, looking down at the altar, seventy feet below. People had indeed died here but, except for unfortunate children, not as sacrificial offerings, but as part of a ritualistic rite believed to forecast the future of the tribe. In the early morning an unlucky individual would be thrown into the cenote. If he survived until noon, he would be rescued; and supposedly having visited the raingod, Chac, he was now prepared to prophesy about the rainfall in the coming year.

"Isn't it lovely?"

"Lovely," he admitted. "And deadly."

"Nothing personal, Sam, but you're a lot easier to take when you're biting my head off." She patted his arm reassuringly. "It's almost time. I promised my source that I'd meet him alone."

His fingers locked around her wrist. "I never agreed to that!"

"Oh, but I did."

"You're crazy," he muttered furiously.

"So you keep telling me. Now if you'll just release me before we draw a crowd, I'll get on with the business of getting my map."

Sam stood his ground. It was his job to protect her, dammit, and he had never been one to shirk his duty.

"I don't like this," he objected. "It's too dangerous."

Davina exhaled a frustrated breath. "Sam," she argued, "take a look around; this place is overrun with tourists. The man wouldn't dare try anything. He'll simply take my money, give me the map and be on his way."

His amber eyes narrowed as they roamed the grounds. "Dammit, Davina—"

"Really, Sam," Davina protested, "you worry too much. I'll be perfectly safe."

He wanted to shout at her, to shake her—anything to keep her from going through with this stunt. Despite every vestige of common sense he possessed, Sam was filled with a dark, uneasy premonition that this place was evil.

"I still don't like it." It irritated him to have his authority questioned.

"Tough," Davina retorted. "If you come with me, you'll ruin everything." She glared up at him, frustrated by the infuriating dark glasses that prohibited her from seeing his eyes. "And if you did that, I'd never forgive you, Sam McGee."

She tugged free of his light restraint and continued toward the crumbled ruins of a sweat house at the edge of the cenote, where ritual purifications had once taken place.

Jamming his hands into his pockets, Sam ground his teeth as he tried to keep an eye on Davina while he scanned the crowds at the same time.

She was no more than fifty feet from him when it happened. Sam watched carefully as a lone man approached Davina, offering a bit of jewelry that gleamed gold in the brilliant sunshine. In turn, he saw Davina take the packet of bank notes from the straw bag she carried over her shoulder. The exchange took no more than sixty seconds, but Sam could not miss the smile of satisfaction that blossomed on Davina's face as she slipped the necklace over her head. The man melded into the clutch of gawking tourists.

Davina turned toward Sam to wave victoriously, when an Indian she had vaguely noticed watching her earlier suddenly bumped against her arm as he passed her on the narrow walkway. Struggling desperately for balance, she teetered precariously on the edge of the well. Before Sam could get to her, Davina had toppled over the edge.

7

As Davina tumbled headlong into space, she heard a frightened voice crying out Sam's name, unaware that it was her own. Seconds later, she plunged into the water, disappearing under the surface, going deeper and deeper until she felt as if her lungs were going to burst. Clutching the medallion around her neck with one hand, she kicked violently in a desperate attempt to return to the surface, to light.

Her vision blurred, stars swam on a backdrop of black velvet as she refused to give in to the dizziness that was threatening to overcome her.

Just when Davina thought she couldn't hold her breath for another heartbeat, her head broke the surface of the water. She gasped, choking water from her lungs as she struggled to regain her breath. Thunder roared in her ears like a summer storm threatening on the horizon. Forcing herself to take several deep, calming breaths as she trod water, Davina looked up, her anxious eyes searching for one man: Sam.

High on the wall, she saw a flurry of activity. The word had obviously spread throughout the site that some foolhardy tourist had fallen into the Well of Sacrifice. Now that her lungs didn't feel like overinflated balloons, Davina's feeling of panic subsided ever so slightly. After all, Sam McGee was somewhere up there in that throng of people; he'd never let her drown.

When he had been forced to watch impotently as Davina disappeared, an iron fist had squeezed his chest in two, giving Sam firsthand knowledge of what a heart attack must feel like. Forbidding himself to dwell on the intense pain shooting through him, he raced to the edge, not realizing that those whispered, desperate prayers were coming from his own lips until Davina's blond head suddenly bobbed to the surface and Sam realized they had been answered.

He cupped his hands around his mouth. "Davina, can you hear me?" When she appeared neither to hear nor to see him, Sam shouted at the gawkers. "Dammit, shut up so I can get her attention!"

There was no one in the group who seemed willing to challenge Sam's authority. Immediately an expectant hush fell over the crowd. Giving them one last blistering glare in warning, Sam tried again.

"Davina? Wave if you can hear me!"

Davina didn't think she'd ever seen anything so beautiful as the sight of Sam, standing so tall, so strong, on the edge of the cenote. At his words, she stopped treading water for a moment in order to follow his instructions. As she lifted her arm out of the water, she went under. A collective gasp rippled through the tourists, followed by a deep sigh of relief as her head became visible again.

"Wait right there," Sam called down to her. "I'll be right back."

She tried to nod, not wanting to experience going under the water again. Seeming to understand, Sam waved his arms encouragingly before turning away and running back toward the Jeep.

Davina continued to slowly move her arms and legs, treading water as she looked around the cenote. Even as frightened as she admittedly was, she couldn't help being struck by the fact that she was now one of a choice group of individuals who had ever viewed it from this angle. When the idea that several of those chosen few had ended up sac-

rificial offerings to Chac—the long-nosed god of rain—
proved decidedly discomforting, she turned her attention
to her immediate surroundings.

A majestic egret sunned himself regally on a clump of
floating twigs, appearing to take her intrusion in stride.
Halfway up the side, two gorgeous birds, blue-green mot-
mots, were engaged in a territorial battle for a limestone
edge. Nearby, a fish broke the surface, appearing like
quicksilver in the blazing sun. The edge of the well was now
lined with curious onlookers, none appearing anxious to do
anything but gaze down in awe of this tourist who had been
foolish enough to fall into the Well of Sacrifice.

Sam encountered little actual opposition to his rescue
plan. In the beginning, a handful of official-looking individuals had made the mistake of foolishly stepping in front
of the Jeep in a futile attempt to stop him from driving
through the site. But when he stepped down on the gas, they
obediently scattered.

He brought the Jeep as close as he could to the edge of the
well and lashed a thick hemp rope onto the length already
coiled around the winch at the front of the vehicle.

"I'm going to throw this rope down to you, Davina!" he
shouted to her. "I want you to loop it under your arms so I
can pull you out of there. Do you understand?"

Davina nodded.

Taking a deep breath, Sam flung the free end of the rope
out over the cenote. It landed with a splash less than three
feet from where Davina was treading water. It only took her
a moment to swim over and wrap it under her arms as he'd
instructed.

"That's the way," he murmured under his breath. "Hang
on, sweetheart, and we'll get you back on solid ground in
no time."

Even as he heard himself saying the words, Sam was forced to admit he was the one he was attempting to reassure, not Davina. The truth was, he had no idea whether his scheme would succeed. He only knew that he could not allow himself to fail. Inch by treacherous inch, he began to lift Davina from the water.

Her ascent up the sheer limestone wall was maddeningly slow, achingly laborious. Once, when she made the mistake of looking down, a never-before-experienced attack of vertigo caused her to become suddenly light-headed. Her body went limp. With the united cry of the crowd ringing in her ears, for one horrifying moment Davina thought she was going to fall back into the well.

As Davina dangled precariously over the blue-green water, Sam struggled to remain outwardly calm while his heart was pounding with a furious, out-of-control rhythm that couldn't possibly have been normal for anyone.

"That's it," he called down encouragingly as she grasped the rope with renewed strength, pushing the soles of her feet against the sheer wall of limestone. "You're doing great."

Well, that was definitely an optimistic overstatement, Davina considered, slumping against a narrow outcropping of stone. Whenever possible, Sam permitted her to stop for a brief rest, but the sides of the cenote were steep, those welcome respites few and far between. But it did seem that she was making steady progress, despite her snaillike pace. Fortunately, the ascent took every bit of her concentration, disallowing her to dwell on her fright.

By the time Davina finally reached the top of the cenote, her arms felt like dead weights and her palms were stinging from the rough hemp rope.

"Don't say anything," Sam warned as he hauled Davina into his arms. His voice was sharp, close to angry.

Earlier, intent on rescuing her, Sam had not let himself think about the risk involved. Except for that initial jolt of panic, he had forced himself to think only of how to get her out of that damned well. He hadn't dared consider the possibility that his efforts might have failed. Now, with her safely on firm ground, fear came slamming into him, harsh and unrestrained. His arms tightened around Davina, and he held her as if he'd never let her go.

"Not one word," he warned, pressing his lips against her wet hair. "Not yet."

Stunned by the obvious emotion in his voice, Davina could only nod. As he carried her back to the Jeep, the crowd parted in respectful waves, like the waters of the Red Sea, allowing them to pass unmolested.

Once she was again on safe ground, the fear that she had managed to control now overcame her. She began to tremble violently, her teeth chattering despite the blazing heat of the Mexican sun.

"Oh, m-m-my God," she groaned into his shoulder, "I thought I was g-going to d-die."

Sam's arms tightened. "I wouldn't have let that happen," he swore with what he knew to be false bravado.

As it was, he had turned out to be one damned poor excuse for a bodyguard. As he put her carefully into the passenger seat of the Jeep, wrapping her in a blanket, Sam was mentally cursing himself in two languages.

As stunned as she was by her near disaster, Davina found herself even more startled by Sam's reaction. She couldn't believe the change in him. During the drive back to Valladolid, he kept looking over at her, as if finding it difficult to believe that she was safe. Davina was admittedly flattered, but his intense scrutiny began to get on her nerves.

Unfortunately, nothing about his demeanor encouraged conversation. He'd retreated behind that brick wall he was able to erect between them, and at the moment, she didn't have the strength to try to breach it.

Sam's heart was still pounding with the intensity of a jackhammer as he tried to sort through his tumultuous thoughts. He didn't think he'd ever forget the sight of Davina falling over the edge of that Sacred Cenote. And it was more than just the usual reaction anyone would have had to such a terrifying situation. The fact that it had been Davina made the entire incident more than horrifying; it had been a nightmare he didn't think he'd ever entirely banish from his mind.

Admittedly he had wanted her from the beginning—from the moment he'd seen her in the doorway of the cantina. In that way, he was forced to acknowledge, his feelings had not been that far removed from Raoul's. She'd been afraid; that much had been obvious. But there had been something in the way she had stiffened her spine, a certain stubborn tilt to her chin, that he'd found undeniably appealing. Later, as he'd begun to gain further insight into her, Sam had witnessed flashes of passion, displays of emotion that only increased his desire.

But something else had happened. Not only did he want Davina, sometime over these past three days, he had come to genuinely like her, as well. Nothing about this woman was turning out to be at all easy. He looked up, as if seeking a solution to his dilemma in the blue sky where dark, angry clouds were beginning to form, forecasting yet another afternoon thunderstorm.

"I think," she said slowly, the rapid-fire chattering of her teeth subsiding as the blanket, as well as the knowledge that she was safe, began to warm her, "that I owe you my life, Sam McGee."

"It was nothing," he said with a forced shrug. "Don't forget, you're—"

"Paying for your services." Her quiet tone was edged with a sadness that tore at some fiber deep inside Sam, despite his effort to remain aloof. "Still, I hired you to be my guide. Not my bodyguard."

The velvet warmth of her voice invited him to soften his attitude, even as Sam reminded himself that he had to stay strong—if not for himself, for her.

Not trusting himself to look at her, he kept his gaze directed at the mirages shimmering just out of reach on the pitted asphalt roadway. "It comes with the territory."

Davina started to speak, but something in the hard set of his jaw stopped the words in her throat. Instead, she reached out, placing her hand on his thigh. The taut muscle stiffened under her fingertips, but he didn't protest. A few miles later, Davina could not stop the smile from blooming on her face when, without a word, Sam covered her slender hand with his.

They remained that way until Sam had parked the Jeep in front of the hotel.

"Stay put," he instructed as she reached out to open her door. A moment later, he had come around the front of the Jeep and scooped her into his arms, blanket and all.

"Sam McGee, put me down," she complained as he carried her to the door. "I'm perfectly capable of walking now."

"The last time I let you call the shots, you almost ended up one more sacrifice to Chac," he countered brusquely.

Despite her sputtered words of protest, he insisted on carrying her up in the elevator to the unabashed interest of the hotel desk clerk and a quartet of elderly men playing checkers at a table in the lobby.

Sam stopped in front of her door. "Give me your key."

His gritty tone did not encourage an argument. Davina obliged, remaining cautiously quiet as he entered the room, kicking her door closed behind him.

He placed her on her feet in the center of the tiled floor, pocketing the brass key. "If you ever pull such a ridiculous stunt again, so help me God, I'll—"

"You'll what?" she challenged, looking up at his granite face. "Beat me?"

His hands cupped her shoulders hard enough to make her wince. "Dammit, Davina," he said on a low note that was more deadly than the loudest roar, "I'm serious."

His mouth was grim, his eyes chips of agate. To a casual observer, it would appear that he was furious with her. But Davina felt she was beginning—albeit barely—to understand this man. As hard as he was on others, Sam McGee would always reserve the toughest standards for himself. And in this case, she had the distinct impression that he was angrier with himself for allowing her to fall into the well in the first place than he was at her for taking the tumble.

She forced herself to meet his blistering gaze with a level look of her own. "I'm exceedingly grateful to you for saving my life, Sam," she said quietly. "However, that doesn't give you the right to yell at me. Or to manhandle me."

He dropped his hands to his sides. "I'm not yelling," he snapped. "I'm trying to force some sense into that crazy head of yours. Don't you realize someone just tried to kill you?"

His harsh words brought an image flashing before Davina's eyes. There had been a man, she recalled suddenly—an Indian with eyes the color of midnight who had watched the surreptitious exchange take place. A fleeting sense of danger had rippled over her when she had viewed the undisguised cruelty in those dark, dangerous eyes. A moment later, she had been falling through space.

At the sudden memory, the shaking started again. "You're wrong." She had to force the words through stiff lips. "It was an accident."

He drew her against him, his hand rubbing against her back in an attempt to soothe her trembling. "I think we both know better than that, Davina."

Davina pressed her cheek against his chest. "No," she whispered. "It couldn't be. Why would anyone want to kill me?"

As soon as she heard herself ask the question, she knew the answer. As she lifted her head, it was all Sam could do not to groan at the excitement washing over the lingering fear in her wide eyes.

"It's because of the map, isn't it?"

"I don't know."

"It is," she insisted. "Don't you see, Sam? This is proof that the map is legitimate!"

He slipped the medallion over her head, tracing the embossed gold figure of an ancient Mayan god-king. For such an ugly thing, it had certainly caused its share of trouble.

"You're jumping to conclusions again," he muttered. "I take it that the infamous map to Naj Taxim is hidden in there."

"Of course it is," she said, eagerly reaching out for the heavy medallion.

Sam caught her hand. "Why didn't you tell me right away that the rope had torn your skin?"

Davina looked down, staring numbly at the red welts crisscrossing her palms. "I hadn't realized it had."

Once again, Sam was furious at himself for not protecting Davina better. He'd only agreed to go on this fool's mission in order to keep her out of danger, and what had happened? Not only had she almost drowned, but thanks to his rescue methods, her skin looked like raw hamburger. He turned her hands over, submitting them to his blistering scrutiny.

"It's not that bad," she argued softly. "And I certainly didn't mean not to hide anything from you. At first I was too frightened to think of anything other than getting out of that well. And then you started talking about attempts on my life, and I remembered that man—"

Every muscle in his body tensed. "What man?"

"An Indian."

"Did he say anything to you? Did he threaten you in any way?"

Davina shook her head. "He didn't say a word. Really, Sam, it was probably nothing but my imagination. It was just his eyes..." Her complexion paled as she vividly recalled that cold, deadly gaze.

"What about his eyes?" Sam demanded.

Davina shook her head to clear it of the still-frightening visage. "It was as if he hated me," she whispered harshly. "But that's ridiculous; I'd never seen him before."

"Would you recognize him if you saw him again?"

Davina shuddered at the thought. "I don't think I'll ever forget him."

She was terrified, Sam realized. Oh, she was making a valiant attempt to hide it, but she was scared to death. And why not? She had had one helluva day. Sam wished that he could hold her in his arms and promise her that everything was going to be all right. But he couldn't—because he had the uneasy feeling such a prediction would only be a lie.

"We'll talk about this later. Right now I need to clean and wrap your hands," he said instead.

She waved away his concern. "You needn't bother; I'm sure they'll be fine."

"Dammit!" Sam exploded. "Just once, would you shut up and not argue with me?"

Davina felt herself growing slowly infuriated by Sam's angry tone. She wondered why it was that all too often her feelings of desire for Sam were comingled with anger. In a strange way, she welcomed her irritation. It steamrollered over heretofore unknown feelings of fear. The strange blend of anger and lingering fear made her words unnecessarily rash.

"I think you're forgetting exactly who's paying for this expedition."

His answering smile was mirthless. "I was waiting for that. This is where you point out that since you're writing the checks, that makes you the boss, right?"

It wasn't easy, facing down his rough, dangerous stance, but Davina gave him a long, challenging look. "I think it's something we should both keep in mind."

Sam realized that her independence meant a great deal to her. After years of obviously living in Jordan Lowell's shadow, she would naturally want to spread her wings and take off on her own. Unfortunately what would have been understandable and acceptable in Boston was not prudent behavior in the Yucatán.

She was going to have to understand that once in awhile it didn't hurt to let someone make the decisions. He had allowed that ridiculous cloak-and-dagger scheme at the ruins, and his compliance almost ended up getting her killed. From now on, Davina was going to have to understand that he was calling all the shots.

He folded his arms over his chest. "You may be footing the bill, but until you demonstrate to me that you've got more in that brain of yours than dry facts from a stack of dusty textbooks, I'm in charge of this expedition. From here on in you'll do what I say, when I say it. With no back talk."

Scarlet flags rose in her cheeks. "I certainly won't agree to that!"

"You don't have any choice."

"I can fire you. And find myself another guide."

FIRST-CLASS ROMANCE

Mail This Heart TODAY!

And We'll Deliver:

4 FREE BOOKS
A FREE MANICURE SET
PLUS
A SURPRISE MYSTERY BONUS
TO YOUR DOOR!

See Inside For More Details →

HARLEQUIN DELIVERS FIRST-CLASS ROMANCE— DIRECT TO YOUR DOOR

Mail the Heart sticker on the postpaid order card today and you'll receive:

—**4 new Harlequin Temptation novels—FREE**
—**a beautiful manicure set—FREE**
—**and a surprise mystery bonus—FREE**

But that's not all. You'll also get:

Money-Saving Home Delivery

When you subscribe to Harlequin Temptation, the excitement, romance and faraway adventures of these novels can be yours for previewing in the convenience of your own home at less than retail prices. Every month we'll deliver 4 new books right to your door. If you decide to keep them, they'll be yours for only $2.24 each. That's 26¢ less per book than what you pay in stores. And there is no extra charge for shipping and handling!

Free Monthly Newsletter

It's the indispensable insider's look at our most popular writers and their upcoming novels. Now you can have a behind-the-scenes look at the fascinating world of Harlequin! It's an added bonus you'll look forward to every month!

Special Extras—FREE

Because our home subscribers are our most valued readers, we'll be sending you additional free gifts from time to time as a token of our appreciation.

OPEN YOUR MAILBOX TO A WORLD OF LOVE AND ROMANCE EACH MONTH. JUST COMPLETE, DETACH AND MAIL YOUR FREE OFFER CARD TODAY!

You'll love your beautiful manicure set—an elegant and useful accessory, compact enough to carry in your handbag. Its rich burgundy case is a perfect expression of your style and good taste—and it's yours free with this offer!

Remember! To receive your free books, manicure set and mystery gift, return the postpaid card below. But don't delay!

DETACH AND MAIL CARD TODAY.

If offer card has been removed, write to: Harlequin Reader Service, 901 Fuhrmann Blvd., P.O. Box 1394, Buffalo, NY 14240-1394

"Go ahead, try it and see what happens," he invited.

Davina's eyes displayed a certain wariness but she held her ground. "Are you threatening me?"

"I'm just stating the facts. And in case you've forgotten, sweetheart, this was all your idea in the first place. I was perfectly contented running my cantina and catching a few fish until you showed up, batting those thick eyelashes and giving me that wide-eyed, cocker-spaniel look until I caved in and let you talk me into some wild-goose chase for a city that doesn't exist and a man who probably bought the farm fifteen months ago. So whether you like it or not, Professor, you're stuck with me, for better or worse, until we either find your father or get proof of his death—whichever comes first."

Sam mentally gave her points for fortitude as she refused to back down. "I've got the map now," she reminded him. "I can probably find Naj Taxim by myself."

"You try to leave this room without me and so help me God, I'll tie you to the bed."

She looked at him suspiciously. "You wouldn't dare."

"I've got lots of rope left."

"You can't keep me a prisoner in here!"

"I can and I will, if that's what it takes to keep you out of trouble."

She shook her head, eyeing him with a mixture of frustration and admiration. "You're something else, McGee."

"Does that mean you're going to behave yourself?"

"It means that I'm willing to take your advice—for now."

Knowing the effort that small capitulation had cost Davina, Sam decided not to push for a total victory. "I'll go down to the Jeep and get the first-aid kit."

He turned in the doorway. "Lock this door while I'm gone," he instructed in a gritty voice that was designed to conceal how desperately he wanted to keep her safe.

Sam knew Davina had been pushed into that well. The question was, by whom? And why? He could only hope that he found the answers before her would-be killer struck again.

He waited outside the door until he heard the twist of the lock. Casting a careful glance in each direction down the hallway, Sam headed toward the fire escape. The stairway would be faster than that ancient elevator; he didn't want to leave Davina alone any longer than was necessary.

By the time Sam was halfway down the hall, Davina's irritation with him had vanished. Instead of wasting time dwelling on Sam McGee's frustratingly arrogant attitude, she turned her attention to the gold filigreed locket the man had given her in exchange for the envelope of money just before she had fallen into the well.

Inside the heavy gold medallion, as promised, Davina found what she was looking for: the map, the legendary map to Naj Taxim—and to her father. As she pressed the piece of parchment against her lips, it was all she could do not to shout for joy.

8

DAVINA STUDIED the map legend carefully, charting mileage. She traced the river the city was supposed to be on with her finger, judging distance and traveling time. With luck, they should have located it before a week was out.

Deep in thought, she failed to hear Sam return to the room. He opened his mouth to warn her to be more attentive when he spotted the piece of parchment in her hand.

"I suppose that's the famous map to Naj Taxim."

Davina nodded.

He expelled a slow breath. "So even after what happened this morning, you're still committed to this search."

At least he hadn't called it a *ridiculous* search, Davina noted. She supposed that was something. "We had a deal," she reminded him quietly. "If I got the map you'd lead me to the city."

"I remember," he said resignedly.

"You'll never believe where the city is."

He could go along with that—since he didn't believe the place existed in the first place. "We'll talk about it after I take care of your hands."

"But—"

He held up a hand to cut her off. "Rule number one," he said in that silky, dangerous tone she had learned to respect. "I set all the rules."

She lifted a questioning brow. "And if I don't agree with rule number one?"

"Tough." He crossed the room to look down at her. "I'm only thinking of you, Davina," he said quietly. "Your health. Your safety. This entire search will be a lot easier if you quit fighting me at every turn."

"I haven't been that bad," she protested.

"Haven't you? I can't remember when I've met a more argumentative female."

Davina smiled at his obvious frustration. It was only the faintest hint of a smile, but it caused his heart to hammer just the same. "Would you believe that most people consider me quite agreeable? That I'm probably the last person at the University anyone would ever accuse of making waves?"

"I'd believe that."

The smile touched her eyes. "Really? After the way you've accused me of behaving?"

He squatted, placing the first-aid kit on the floor beside him. Davina didn't offer a word of protest as he took her hand. He frowned as he studied the deep red welts.

"Most people don't know you," he said mildly. He began rubbing some cooling, green gel over her palm.

How strange that such large hands could be so tender, Davina mused. Those strong dark hands that could excite her body with the slightest touch were now caressing her skin with a gentleness she never would have thought Sam McGee capable of.

"And you do—" she challenged softly "—know me?"

He looked up from his ministrations, meeting the myriad of questions in her aquamarine eyes with a steady look. "I'm beginning to feel as if I'd known you all my life," he said simply.

In a way it was true. Sam was beginning to realize that he had been subconsciously anticipating Davina Lowell's arrival for a very long time. The remarkable thing was that he hadn't even realized it until she had walked uninvited and unannounced into his life.

Davina could think of no words to answer Sam's startling admission. She fell silent, watching as he continued spreading the soothing gel over her hands before wrapping them in white gauze.

"That does feel a lot better," she admitted when he had finished the task.

"It's aloe vera. The sting'll be gone in about twenty minutes. It should keep your hands from swelling, and with any luck, tomorrow the redness will be gone. If they don't look a lot better, we'll take you to the doctor."

"Tomorrow we're going to Naj Taxim," she reminded him.

"That's where you're wrong; tomorrow we're staying right here."

"Here?" She didn't bother to keep the grievance from her tone. "Why?"

He put away the gauze and gel and closed the lid of the first-aid kit decisively. "Because we're not leaving town until I know for certain those cuts aren't going to get infected. There aren't a lot of drugstores in the jungle, Davina. I'm not going to let you risk blood poisoning along with everything else."

"For heaven's sake, Sam," she retorted, "I'm not an invalid. Or a baby. You don't have to coddle me."

He touched her cheek, his strong, gentle fingers just brushing over her skin. "Would it kill you to let someone take care of you for a change?"

A simple enough question, but Davina realized that it was staggering in its implications. When had been the last time anyone had taken care of her, catered to her? Her father had always been busy—locked in his study, or halfway around the world leading his archaeological teams to exciting new discoveries.

Her aunt, Jordan Lowell's elder sister, had taken in her brother's child as an act of sibling obligation. But even though she had tried, Davina's aunt could not change her own nature. Harriet Lowell had never been a demonstrative person, and the arrival of a seven-year-old child at her venerable Louisville Square home had not lessened her reserve.

As a result, Davina had learned at an early age to be strong and emotionally self-sufficient. It had been clear that her father preferred her that way. And Davina had always done her best to be a model daughter to her beloved, larger-than-life parent. She was still trying, she had to admit to herself.

"I'm quite used to taking care of myself," she said at length.

Sam nodded. "I'm sure you are. But I've never had an opportunity to pamper anyone, Davina. What would you say to trying it for twenty-four hours and seeing how we like it?"

"Twenty-four hours? That's all?"

"Unless those hands get infected. Then we'll have to re-negotiate."

Actually, despite her desire to reach the city as soon as possible, the idea of a single day to do whatever she pleased, without deadlines, schedules or obligations, sounded like nirvana.

"I think you're a bad influence on me," she said with a shaky little laugh. "Because I'm tempted to do exactly that."

Humor came into his eyes. "That's my girl."

"Woman," she corrected absently, automatically.

"My woman."

Sam's tone was light and easy, but there was something about those particular words that caught them both by surprise. Sam looked as surprised to have uttered the possessive statement as Davina had been to hear it, and for a moment they simply stared at each other while the implication hovered in the air between them.

"I think you'd better show me the map now," Sam said finally.

Davina's eyes remained on his shuttered face, searching for secrets. Nothing. Absolutely nothing. So what else was new? She handed him the tissue-thin piece of parchment without a word.

He swore. "The Usumacinta River? Give me a break, Davina."

"I'll admit it isn't the most accessible place—"

"What the hell are you trying to do?" he broke in roughly. "Get us killed? Wasn't that little escapade this morning dangerous enough for you?"

"Really, Sam," Davina said soothingly, "aren't you exaggerating? Just a little?"

"Are you calling boiling rapids and dangerous currents exaggerating?" he shot back. "How about so many armed guerrillas running around that jungle that you need a scorecard to keep track of who's shooting at you? And let's not forget the bandits from the refugee camps. Which of those little items do you consider an exaggeration?"

He was standing over her, gripping her shoulders more firmly than necessary. "This isn't a game, Davina. It isn't some fraternity scavenger hunt. We're talking about life and death here, lady."

"I know that!" she shouted back, pushing ineffectually against his chest. "In case you've forgotten, it's my father's life I'm trying to save!"

Sam was seconds away from shaking her until her teeth rattled. Unwilling to surrender control, he snatched his hands from her shoulders, shoving them with violent force into his pockets.

"For once in your life," he suggested between clenched teeth, "why don't you stop putting your father first and think of yourself?"

He'd struck a raw nerve with that one. Vowing not to cry, Davina tossed her head furiously. "I suppose I should expect that advice from you. Since it's more than obvious that you don't ever think of anyone *but* yourself. And probably never have."

Watching a dark color rise under his tan, Davina realized her reckless shot had hit the mark. Sam appeared on the brink of exploding, and she knew that the prudent thing to do would be to back away from this now. But fury and frustration conspired to make her more daring than usual.

"That's what you're doing down here in this pesthole of a place, isn't it?" she inquired scathingly. "The real world requires a little cooperation, some thoughtfullness—even love. But you wouldn't understand any of that."

Her eyes frosted as they raked over him. "You've been away from civilization so long, McGee, that you wouldn't recognize a decent human emotion if it was staring you in the face."

Sam was absolutely rigid, utilizing every ounce of strength he possessed to keep from losing his temper and doing something he'd regret. Davina wasn't telling him anything he hadn't told himself a million times. But hearing such accusations from her hurt more than he could have ever imagined in his most brutal nightmares.

"Are you finished yet?" he asked finally, as she stopped to take several deep, calming breaths.

There was something about those amber eyes, hard yet strangely wounded in his stony face, that proved to be Davina's undoing. She turned away.

"For now."

"You're right, you know."

She stared unseeingly out the window. "I overreacted."

"No. You said exactly what you were feeling, what needed to be said. And you were right. I have been away too long; I probably have forgotten the right things to say, the way to say them. All those little pleasantries people—women—expect."

She slowly turned toward him, her aquamarine eyes filled with contrition. "Sam—"

He had his hand on the doorknob, prepared to leave. "You're free to get yourself another guide. But there's something you should know first."

Shaking her head, Davina tried again. "I don't want—"

"When I said the river was too dangerous, I was only thinking of you. I'm not a man to pretty things up with poetry and flowers, Davina, but since we seem to be speaking our minds, you should know that I haven't stopped thinking of you since I first saw you."

She opened her mouth to respond, but couldn't force the words past the sudden lump in her throat.

"I'm not saying that all those thoughts have been flattering," he added with that brutal candor that she was beginning to respect. "Sometimes I wanted to wring your neck. But there hasn't been an hour—hell, there haven't been five minutes—when thoughts of you haven't taken over my mind."

He turned then, opening the door to leave. "Lock this behind me," he instructed. Then he was gone.

Davina sank wearily onto the bed, for the first time aware of the stinging pain flashing across her palms. She was suddenly very tired. And frustrated. And more than a little discouraged. But she knew it was one of those things that made her want to weep.

THE KNOCK AT THE DOOR woke Davina from a restless slumber. Exhausted by her misadventure that morning, followed by the heated argument with Sam, she had fallen asleep on top of the woven bedspread. The room was deep in shadows, giving evidence of the fact that it was evening.

If she was upset by their argument, Davina was appalled at how her spirits lifted at the thought that Sam had returned. She flung open the door, her welcoming smile instantly fading as she viewed a young woman carrying a dinner tray.

"*Buenas tardes,*" the woman said with a smile.

"*Buenas tardes.*" The aroma rising from the tray reminded Davina that she hadn't eaten yet today. "That smells wonderful, but I didn't order anything," she said regretfully.

The waitress looked past her into the room, as if asking permission to enter. Davina belatedly realized that she obviously didn't speak English. Her own Spanish a little rusty from years of disuse, she tried again to explain that the woman obviously had the wrong room, but the waitress stood firm.

"*El señor,*" she said, followed by a rush of words that although Davina could not translate precisely left no doubt as to who had ordered the dinner.

"Come in. *Adelante.*" Davina moved aside, inviting her into the room. The waitress placed the tray on the dresser, thanked Davina for the generous tip and wished her a pleasant evening. It was only after she had left the room that Davina noticed the envelope beside the dinner plate.

"Eat every bit of this meal. We've got a rough trip ahead of us; you're going to need all your strength."

Despite the gritty tone of the directive, Davina couldn't help but smile. She supposed, in a way, this could be considered pampering. As Sam himself had admitted, he hadn't had a great deal of practice. Succumbing to the tantalizing aroma, she settled down to the dinner of grilled whitefish, fruit and rice, finding the taste every bit as delicious as the aroma.

DESPITE A LIGHT SLEEP filled with discomforting thoughts of Sam McGee, Davina woke with a renewed sense of optimism about her quest. She had the map. And she had Sam. She would not allow herself to consider the unpalatable prospect of failure.

She was taking a bath in the ancient, claw-footed tub when she slowly became aware of someone else in the room. Lifting her eyes, she was not surprised to view Sam leaning against the doorjamb. It had not escaped her notice that in his aggravation he had failed to return her key last night. Although she hated admitting it, she had spent the better part of the night waiting for him to return.

"I knocked, but you didn't answer."

She tried to match his even tone. "I probably didn't hear you over the running water."

He nodded gravely. "That was probably the case." He hesitated the slightest heartbeat of a second, as if considering his words carefully. "I was afraid you'd left."

Her lashes swept down and her fingers tightened on the bath sponge. "I couldn't do that."

He felt a vague desire for a cigarette and ignored it. She was right about one thing. He smoked too much. One of these days he was going to have to face that fact. But not today. Today his mind was on other things—such as ignoring the ache swelling inside him at the sight of Davina sitting amid those fragrant bubbles.

"So you're still determined to go through with this."

Davina's only response was a slight nod of her head. She decided that it was better that he'd misinterpreted her words. What she had meant by her softly stated admission was that she couldn't leave him. Not now. Not until they'd resolved whatever there was between them.

She picked up a bar of soap from the tiled holder and worked up a thick, creamy lather between her palms. "You were right about the aloe vera," she stated in a feigned, conversational tone as she worked the lather up her arms. "My hands are much better this morning."

Sam recognized the scent immediately and was surprised to learn that the evocative perfume that had been driving him crazy for days was nothing more than Ivory soap. Ivory soap and her own inimitable feminine fragrance. Another desire rose hot and tenacious, overriding the vague need for a cigarette.

"This is impossible, you realize," he murmured.

"The expedition?" she asked, knowing better.

He managed a smile as he shook his head. "No, not the expedition."

He entered the bathroom, breathing in the warm fragrant mist that brought to mind a tropical rain forest. Bubbles covered the surface of the water, but they couldn't entirely shield her from his slow, appreciative gaze. Rosy nipples jutted through the frothy suds covering her breasts. Her hair was piled precariously atop her head. He had a sudden urge to press his lips against her slender throat.

"You look delicious." He squatted beside her.

Unbidden, the desire that was never far away sprang up between them, so palpable that Davina felt as if she could reach out and touch it. She swallowed.

"Really?"

Sam glanced down at the creamy breasts, satisfied as he watched the ripe little buds harden in response to his softly drawled compliment. "Really. You remind me of something they serve up at Dairy Queen."

A flush moved over the soft flesh visible above the bubbles. "I'm not blushing," Davina said firmly, hating the warmth she felt flowing under her skin.

"Of course not," Sam agreed easily.

"I never blush," she insisted, glancing around, satisfied that the bubbles were still providing some modesty.

"I believe you." He plucked the sponge from her nerveless fingers and dunked it under the suds. "Turn around."

"What are you doing?"

His eyes didn't move from hers. "Washing your back."

"I don't remember asking you to do that."

"Of course you did."

He squeezed the sponge over her shoulder, watching as the perfumed water ran over the slope of her breast, taking a wide swath of frothy bubbles with it.

"You ask me to touch you every time you look at me with those wide, turquoise eyes; whenever you smile at me with those soft, inviting lips."

He trailed a finger down the path the water had made. "Every time your skin flames when I touch you—here—and here."

Shaken, Davina dropped the soap. "Now you've made me lose it," she complained, searching around under the water.

"That's the advantage of this stuff," he countered smoothly. "It floats."

Before Davina could utter a word of protest, Sam's hands had dived under the layer of bubbles, capturing the plump white bar of soap. A moment later, he casually lifted her leg out of the water.

"Have I mentioned that you've got great legs?" He ran the slippery bar from her ankle, over her calf, up her thigh.

Davina was melting under his tantalizing touch. "No."

"You do; they're firm, shapely. You must be an exercise fiend."

"I ride a bike," she managed with a gasp as his fingers skimmed treacherously close to that secret point that throbbed with aching need. "There's a group of us at the university." Arousal simmered, making coherent thought difficult. "We put on bikeathons to raise money for charity."

"I figured it was something like that." Sam lowered her leg to the water, repeating the same tantalizing torture with the other. "Do you really have a black belt in karate?"

Did the man know he was driving her crazy? Of course he did, Davina decided, vowing that she'd pay Sam McGee back for every nerve he was presently shattering.

"No," she said raggedly as she began to squirm, reaching for that taunting hand. "I lied."

"I thought as much." Underneath the water, Sam obliged her to a point as his fingers brushed through the soft blond curls at the apex of her thighs.

Frustrated beyond belief, Davina captured his hand. "You're right, this is impossible." She tilted her chin ever so slightly as she studied the desire burning like molten gold in his eyes.

"You want me," she diagnosed softly. "But you don't want to want me."

She was not only lovely, but perceptive, as well. Sam wondered how willing Davina would be to make love with him if she knew the truth about his past.

"Does it matter?"

To Sam's surprise, she appeared to be seriously considering the question. Desire pounded within him as he waited for her answer. He knew that he would adhere to Davina's decision if she opted to stop things here and now, but he also knew that walking away from her would be the hardest thing he'd ever done.

"It should," she admitted finally with a slight, barely perceptible inclination of her head. Although his eyes were locked onto hers, Sam could sense the rise and fall of her breasts as she breathed a slight, somewhat regretful sigh. "But it doesn't."

Confusion warred with need in the aquamarine depths of her eyes. "Why don't I feel as if I have any choice about this?"

She had always mapped out her life carefully, to the last detail. It was coming as an unpleasant surprise that some things—and some men—could not be planned for.

"Because you don't," he said simply.

At his matter-of-fact tone, Davina felt a flush of anger. A moment later his hand was gentle as it touched her face. "There's never been any choice, Davina. For either of us."

With a tenderness that was at direct odds with the dark passion on his face, Sam lifted Davina from the velvet cling of water, carrying her to the bed.

"The sheets," she murmured distractedly, "they'll get wet."

"Forget the sheets." His fingers traced a line of fire down her throat and around each breast, leaving sparks on her skin.

Davina reached up and slid her arms around his neck and smiled. "Consider them forgotten." She tangled her fingers in his dark hair, pulling his head down to her lips. "Kiss me," she demanded in a soft, throaty voice.

He brushed his lips teasingly against hers. "With pleasure."

She tightened her grip on the back of his head. "No," she protested against his mouth. "Really kiss me."

He cupped her breasts in his hands, his thumbs brushing against her nipples as he gave her a long, deep, open-mouthed kiss that escalated the throbbing ache in his loins. She tasted delicious. Sweet. Tempting. Forbidden.

Unable to resist, he trailed his lips down her body, plucking at her warm skin, exploring her pliant body with sexy, moist kisses. He was rapidly discovering that Davina affected him as an aphrodisiac would; the more he tasted, the hungrier he became.

Davina felt as if she were floating, unable to deny Sam anything as he turned her in his arms to press stinging little kisses down her back. Electricity danced between the delicate bones of her spine. When his fingers curved on her firm buttocks, massaging her flesh, she moaned into the soft down pillow.

Desperate to feel her body against his, Sam managed to dispense with his clothes with one hand; the other never stopped its seductive caresses, moving from her neck to the back of her knees.

"You're incredible," he said huskily, lowering his body carefully onto hers. The flames that had been flickering between them flared at the heated contact. "Where have you been all my life?"

"Boston," she whispered, turning her head so she could recapture those wonderful lips. "I've been in Boston."

"I think I've finally found something to love about Boston." As his hands slipped between them, Sam found her warm and wet, ready for him. His fingers deftly parted the soft pink flesh, gently stroking her petaled softness until she was crying out for fulfillment.

Davina's body burned and so did Sam's as he continued to fondle her, loving the way she held nothing back. She seemed to bloom under his loving touch, her skin flushed with a soft pink glow. Sam knew that he had never seen anything quite as lovely as Davina at that moment. The pins had come out of her hair, and he buried his face in the flowing golden waves as he thrust forward, unable to hold back another moment.

Davina cried out as he claimed her, unaware that she was saying Sam's name over and over as their bodies moved in unison. They were ruthless, driving each other to the brink of madness with an urgency unlike anything they had ever known. A flood of passion stormed over Sam, sweeping away the last vestiges of his control, and he closed his eyes as he gave himself up to its power.

Davina felt Sam's body stiffen, then shudder. An instant later he touched her and she followed him over the edge.

THEY LAY TOGETHER, legs tangled, arms wrapped around each other as their breathing returned to normal. *Now what?* Sam asked himself as he unconsciously pressed his lips against the top of her head. Where in the hell did they go from here?

Although it was true that he had wanted Davina from the first, Sam had never planned to feel so strongly about her. For the first time in five years he found himself involved in something over which he had no control, and he didn't like the feeling. She had invaded the most intimate reaches of his mind; he couldn't think of an instance in the past four days when he had been able to completely shut her out of his thoughts. Even now, even when he should be experiencing a feeling of satisfaction, Sam discovered that he wanted more.

Davina felt Sam's sigh and dared a cautious glance upward. His mouth was set in that all-too-familiar grim line, but there was no mistaking the tenderness in his eyes.

"I told you we'd get the sheets wet," she said with a soft, encouraging smile.

She was too damned trusting. If she was left to her own devices, there was no telling what trouble the woman would get herself into. Sam told himself that was the only reason he was agreeing to see this insane search to the end. He couldn't allow himself to believe anything else.

"So we'll spend the day in my bed." He tilted her chin up and kissed her mouth.

"All day?" she asked against his mouth.

He tangled his fingers in the soft waves trailing over her shoulders, luxuriating in the soft scent, the silken texture. "We agreed that this was going to be Pamper Davina Lowell Day, remember?"

Merry lights danced in her eyes. "All day? Are you sure you're up to that?" she challenged, trailing a provocative finger down his torso.

"Try me."

His strong, wide hands moved down her back as his lips nibbled hers and Davina found herself being seduced by him all over again. She wanted him—now. But first there was something she had to know.

"Did you mean it?"

"Mean what?" As her satiny skin warmed under his touch, Sam's loins stirred with renewed hunger.

She trembled as he traced a seductive path up the inside of her thigh with his square-cut fingernail. "That you'd stay with me. Until I found Naj Taxim."

"Until Naj Taxim," he agreed, pulling her onto him in one smooth, deft motion.

Well, it wasn't forever. But it was enough—for now. As their bodies joined, Davina stopped thinking.

9

"IF WE KEEP THIS UP," Sam groaned a great deal later, "I'm going to make one lousy guide. You'll have to carry me to Naj Taxim."

Davina's fingers were playing in the ebony curls covering his chest. "You sound as if you believe it really exists," she said carefully.

"I wish I did—for your sake."

Davina didn't know whether to be pleased that Sam had just revealed that he cared for her, or depressed that he still didn't believe in her mission.

"Would you like to see the map? So we can plan our strategy?"

Heaving a deep sigh of resignation, he hitched himself up in the bed, bringing Davina with him. "Since you're paying me all that dough in order to be your guide, I suppose the map might be in order."

She pressed a swift, hard kiss against his lips. "Even if we never find the city, Sam, you've been well worth the money."

She left the bed to retrieve the map from the dresser. When she turned around, Sam's expression was anything but encouraging.

"I don't think I like the idea of being a gigolo."

Davina couldn't help herself. She burst out laughing.

"I don't find anything so damn funny about our situation," he complained.

Her eyes brimmed with tears of laughter. Sam—her strong, virile, magnificent Sam—resembled a sulky little boy who had just gotten his shiny red Christmas bicycle taken away from him. She sat on the edge of the bed and brushed at the nerve jerking ominously in his cheek with her fingertip.

"I was only teasing, Sam."

He eyed her dubiously. "That isn't anything to joke about. My God, Davina, don't you remember how you felt when I thought you were nothing but a hooker?"

"Of course I remember. I was flattered."

"What?"

She smiled at him. "Though I'll admit that I wasn't thrilled with you thinking that I'd ply my trade in a dump like the cantina—"

"Dump?" he interrupted, arching a challenging black brow.

"Well, it isn't exactly The Ritz, Sam. Anyway, I'll have to admit it was rather nice of you to believe that I could actually make a living selling my body."

His eyes took a slow, intimate tour of the female body in question. "You're a little skinny," he said truthfully, running a rough palm down her side. "But every ounce is prime."

Her eyes sparkled with amusement. "Why, Sam McGee, you certainly know how to sweet-talk a girl off her feet." She gave him a long, lingering kiss.

"I don't know why I agreed to this expedition in the first place," he complained as they came up for air. "You're going to drive me crazy, Davina Lowell."

"I'm certainly going to try." Her hands skimmed down his back.

Sam's irritation melted under the warm, laughing lights in Davina's eyes. "Let me see that map," he said with obvious reluctance. He gave her a rakish grin. "After that, I refuse to be held responsible for any naughty ideas you come up with."

Davina watched silently as Sam studied the map. Frowns carved deep furrows in his brow, and every so often he'd mutter a curse under his breath. All in all, she considered, his attitude was anything but encouraging.

"There's a good-size airfield at Palenque," he said finally, pointing at the location on another map, one of the entire peninsula and adjoining area that he'd retrieved from his own room. "We'll fly in there tomorrow."

"And then?"

He exhaled a deep breath. "I don't suppose there's anything I can say or do to get you to change your mind." One look at Davina's face told its own story. "I didn't think so," he muttered.

He spread out the larger chart on the mattress between them, placing her map next to it. "All right, here's the Usumacinta."

Davina repeated the name, unfamiliar with the accent that was not quite Spanish. "What does it mean?"

He shrugged. "Who knows. It's an Indian name—the meaning's been lost in antiquity. Perhaps you can find the answer in that ancient text of yours that described Naj Taxim so well."

"There you go, being sarcastic again," Davina said huffily. "I only asked a simple question. Would it have been too difficult to give me a simple, civil answer?"

"Nothing's simple about you, sweetheart."

From his tone, Davina couldn't quite tell if she'd been insulted or not. She opted not to challenge the statement; last night's argument had left her afraid that Sam would wash his hands of the entire mission and return to Chetumal. She didn't want that to happen—for many complicated reasons.

"And this is Yaxchilán," she murmured, returning her attention to the map, pointing to an archaeological site not far from where Naj Taxim supposedly was built. "I've always wanted to visit those ruins."

Sacred to the local Lacandon Indians, who believed their Mayan ancestors lived there, the temples of Yaxchilán had weathered twelve centuries of tropical rains. The forest in the region was also named for the Lacandon; over the centuries the name had become synonymous with impenetrability. Sam wondered which of them was crazy—Davina for thinking up this wild-goose chase, or himself for agreeing to go along with it. He decided they both were.

"I wasn't aware that this was a sight-seeing trip."

She glanced up at him, curious as to the reason for his gruff tone. The blatant concern in his eyes had her immediately dropping her gaze back to the pair of maps.

"I just thought that if we were in the vicinity—"

Shaking his head in a mute display of disgust at himself for upsetting her again, Sam covered her hand with his. "We'll try to fit it in."

"Only if it won't take up too much time." She was quick to qualify. Despite the fact that she didn't want their time together to end quickly, she could not discount his daily fee. She didn't want to think of what today was costing her.

His fingers squeezed hers reassuringly. "We'll fit it in," he promised. "My treat."

Her response was a breathtakingly brilliant smile. "Thank you, Sam."

"You know," he felt obliged to point out, "the fact that your map shows Naj Taxim to be somewhere between the Planchon de las Figuras and Yaxchilán only serves to discount the entire legend. People have traipsed all over that part of the jungle. How do you explain them overlooking an entire city?"

"Río Azul was built in the eighth century and covers 750 acres," she said. "And it wasn't surveyed and excavated until this decade. And don't forget Tikal. It was locked in the thick of Guatemala's jungle for a thousand years before it was discovered."

"But it was known about for years," Sam argued. "Anyone flying over it could see those five stone roof-combs protruding above the forest. There have never been any sightings of Naj Taxim."

"It's obviously not as tall."

He threw his hands in the air, signaling defeat. "You're a dreamer."

The look Davina gave him was immeasurably solemn. "I don't have any choice."

Sam studied her for a long, silent moment. "No," he said finally, "I don't suppose you do."

He continued to map out the plan, pointing out villages along the river that formed the border between Guatemala and Mexico that they could use as base camps for expeditions on foot into the jungle.

"We'll start up the river at Baco Lacantún," he decided. "It's the only place where we can get to that part of the river by roadway. From there we'll travel the Lacantún to where it merges with the Usumacinta by raft." Then, as if as an afterthought, he asked, "You can do more than tread water, can't you?"

"Want to see my Red Cross badge?"

"I'll take your word for it. I just don't want to have to go diving into the river to pull you out of the jaws of some crocodile."

Davina repressed the sliver of fear that skimmed up her spine. "Don't worry," she said with a calm assurance she was a long way from feeling, "you won't have to."

He nodded his acceptance. "Good."

Sam's expression softened, and he reached out and twisted her hair around his finger. He started to speak, then stopped himself. Davina waited.

He could see the unspoken question on her face. She had given herself to him today—unhesitatingly, eagerly. With a passion he had suspected all along she possessed, Davina had held nothing back. He owed her a great deal. Although he could never be what she deserved, he could at least give her something in return. He could, in some small way, let her know how important she had become to him in such a short time.

"I would, you know."

The strange, serious look in his eyes tore at some delicate fiber deep inside Davina. She pressed her palm against his cheek. "I know," she whispered.

They held each other then and for a time, it was enough.

IF DAVINA HAD CONSIDERED Sam at all lazy, the next three days were to prove her wrong. Gone was the unenterprising cantina owner, and in his place was a dynamic, nononsense man who flew the rental plane himself to Palenque, bartered mercilessly for supplies and brooked no argument from underhanded government officials as he arranged for the papers that would allow them to explore both banks of the river—the Mexican side and the Guatemalan bank.

At night, alone in their hotel room, Sam was the same ardent, considerate lover capable of taking her to unexplored heights of passion. But now that she had seen him in action, Davina found herself even more curious about his past life—before the Yucatán; before her.

"Oh, look!" Davina exclaimed, stopping at a craftsman's booth outside the hotel on the morning they left for the river.

"We've got everything we need, sweetheart." Right now, Sam wanted nothing more than to get to Boca Lacantún and begin the absurd scavenger hunt.

"But, Sam," she argued, unable to resist the hopeful look on the face of the young vendor who couldn't have been more than eight years old, "surely just one more thing wouldn't swamp the raft."

Her hurried gaze swept over the display of brightly lacquered trays and bowls. "This one," she decided, picking up a gourd that had been transformed into an ornate bowl by repeated rubbings with oil, earth and pigment. A wonderworld of nature embellished the crimson and ebony exterior.

She held it up for Sam's perusal. "Isn't it perfect?"

"Perfect," he muttered. "Davina, we really need to be going."

She flashed him a brilliant smile. "Just one more second," she promised.

Sam resisted interfering as Davina asked the cost, then immediately paid the price.

"You're supposed to barter," he said as they drove toward the river.

Davina was tracing the elaborate design with her finger. "I know. But I never can do it."

"I still contend you're a chump," he said, the smile softening his words. "A lovely one, granted, but a chump just the same."

"It was a ridiculously low price," she argued. "Besides, you have to admit, I was right about the map."

"You were right about the guy having a map to sell," Sam agreed. "However, we've yet to establish proof that it's anything but an elaborate hoax—one the guy's managed to pull off two times that we know of.

"By the way," he said, not giving her a chance to argue that point, "while the map is probably counterfeit, the man just happened to be for real. I don't think he had anything to do with your fall into the cenote."

Davina's irritation evaporated. She looked over at him curiously. "How on earth do you know that?"

Sam waved to a small, ragtag group of Indians on their way to Friday market. The farmers trudged along, as they had since the days of antiquity, the traditional net bags swinging from tumplines around their foreheads.

"Luis has a cousin, Alejandro, who works for the government, tracking down stolen artifacts. According to him, your map salesman had more aliases than he does scruples. But although he dealt regularly in smuggled artifacts, he wasn't known for killing off his customers."

"Then you believe it was just an accident?" she asked hopefully.

"I don't think so, since Luis called me this morning with the additional news that the guy was found dead only a few hours after he handed the map over to you."

Davina felt the short hairs at the back of her neck bristle at the unsavory news. "I don't suppose you're going to tell me he died of natural causes."

"He was lying facedown in an alley with a knife in his back."

"This is dangerous country," she insisted. "There are probably lots of people who'd kill for a handful of pesos— let alone five thousand dollars."

"Granted," Sam acknowledged grimly. "But I still think it's too much of a coincidence. Don't forget your Indian with the angry eyes."

"The part about his eyes could have simply been my imagination," she argued.

"And he could have been trying to kill you."

Davina felt the beginnings of a headache coming on. Under normal conditions, she hated any talk of killing. When the subject concerned herself, it was doubly unpalatable.

"Why would he want to do that?"

Sam shrugged. "Who knows? Perhaps he had a buyer of his own for the map—one who was willing to pay more."

An idea that had been flickering at the far reaches of her mind for the past three days suddenly became crystal clear. "Or he could be trying to keep me from reaching Naj Taxim."

Sam had admittedly thought of that one. But it didn't make any sense—since the city was nothing but an appealing fable in the first place.

"I think that fall must have damaged your brain," he muttered, wishing he could find the key that would enable him to keep Davina safe for the rest of this ridiculous trek. "We should probably stop at the nearest doctor and have your head examined for holes."

"You're just mad because I thought of a better reason than you did."

"I'm not mad."

"You could have fooled me," she mumbled, her voice cooling slightly.

"I thought you were an educated woman. Dogs get mad. Coyotes get mad. Even squirrels. But not me."

Davina arched an argumentative blond brow. She was in no mood for a vocabulary lesson. "So what do you call your all-too-frequent lapses into ill temper?"

"I'll admit that from time to time I get annoyed," he said. "Irritated, perhaps."

She had to laugh at that. "And you're also the master of understatement."

Sam's crooked, acknowledging grin demonstrated how far they had come in the past week. Seven days ago, her light accusation would have earned a blistering glare. Today, he merely shrugged.

The trip to Boca Lacantún was uneventful, save for the interesting fact that many of the Indians in the region appeared to know Sam intimately. They greeted him with shouts and waves as the Jeep bucked along the dirt roadway. They brought him baskets of fruit, showed off babies obviously born since his last trek into the jungle, and posed proudly for pictures.

As Davina realized that Sam had developed a strange sort of kinship with these people, she began to accept the fact that he belonged here. If it had been difficult for her to picture Sam McGee in Philadelphia or Boston or Manhattan before, it was now an impossibility.

They had been on the Lacantun River about thirty minutes when they approached a giant sheet of limestone sloping into the river from the jungle-choked banks. The slab, carved with the graffiti of Maya traders, depicted animals, including a strange, striding monkeylike creature, humans, mysterious spirals and temples.

"We could stop," Sam offered as Davina stared in wonder at the Planchon de las Figuras—flatiron with figures.

She glanced around at the boatmen squatting on the flat rocks beside their dugouts. Some were cooking small river fish, others were playing board games, a few simply traded stories. She couldn't help but think that the scene probably didn't look all that different from the time when the Maya traders used the site as a commercial center. Near a major river junction, it was a place where cool springwater could be found and boatmen could while away the hours much as these men did today.

"No," she said with regretful sigh. "If we stop at every site, we'll never get to Naj Taxim."

"Next time," Sam suggested.

"Next time," she agreed, knowing as she did so that there would never be a next time.

Come the end of August, whether she had found Naj Taxim and her father or not, she was expected back at Boston University to begin the new semester.

Sam watched the shadow come and go in her eyes. They both knew there would be no next time, but for some reason it had seemed important to pretend otherwise.

For a time Davina felt disoriented by their direction—the Usumacinta flowed north—an oddity among rivers in North America—but soon she adjusted and found the Lacandón forest, in its pristine state, almost cathedrallike.

Not that any cathedral would ever be so hot. Few sunbeams penetrated the sweltering shade, and at ground level no breeze stirred. In the stifling heat minutes seemed like hours, and Davina's clothes were clinging to her drenched skin as they rafted under a dense canopy of tropical trees—chicle, mahogany, cedar, sapodilla, kapok and palm—covered with climbing and air-growing plants. She stared into the nearly impenetrable tangle of vines and greenery and wished she could learn the secrets that the trees were so effectively shielding.

Water fell down in a number of wide cascades amid the luxuriant tropical vegetation; the falls looked appealing, but she knew that to stop and plunge into the tumbling falls would only be wasting precious time. Repressing a shiver at the sight of crocodiles basking lazily on the banks, she cast a quick, reassuring glance at the steel-blue automatic pistol Sam wore in a tooled-leather holster.

"They're mostly harmless," he said, having watched her eyes move from the reptiles to his hip. "Once in awhile they'll come up to the raft to check us out, but you don't have to worry about them climbing aboard. They aren't any more eager to tangle than you are."

"Try telling that to the crocodiles," she murmured.

His grin was quick, wide and devastating. "I have. But I still wouldn't advise trailing your fingers in the water."

They continued downstream in a suffocating humidity that subdued all sounds save for the hum of the raft's engine and the powerful swish of the current against jagged limestone rocks. Every so often Sam would point out a sight—a colorful red macaw hidden in the foliage, a fat turtle sleeping on a log—and Davina would marvel at the quantity of life the jungle sustained.

Late in the day, as the river cut like a knife through a mountain spur, she heard a low roar—a distant rumble like a freight train—and glanced up, looking for the storm clouds that would call a halt to their progress.

"It's not thunder," Sam said, bending down to check the ties on her life jacket.

When she had first seen the slow, muddy river, she had objected to wearing the bulbous orange vest, but Sam had been insistent. She was about to find out why.

"Then what—"

"We're in for a stretch of white water. Hang on tight."

As the roar grew louder, she could not disguise the raw fear she was feeling. Her heart was beating a mile a minute, and her mouth went dry. Her knuckles were chalk white as she gripped the splash guard.

Sam squeezed her shoulder reassuringly. "Don't worry, it always sounds terrifying, but the sound is a lot worse than the run itself."

"That's easy for you to say," Davina muttered, her heart in her throat.

As they came around a bend, the rubber raft was suddenly swept away by the surging current. The bow of the raft rose, like a roller-coaster car, to the water's crest. Unable to do otherwise, Davina closed her eyes as the raft dipped abruptly and dropped back into the churning white water. When the bow slapped into the trough, water came from every direction. Waves whipped in, drenching her to the skin as the raft bounced and bucked like a wild bronco. The water exploded over them, hissing and bubbling, the maelstrom tossing and turning them like a piece of cork on a stormy sea.

Wave after wave broke in her face; the raft slid down into the V of one particularly deep wave and water landed in her lap. Another followed, and another, until they were swamped. Despite the careful job Sam had done strapping down the supplies, several boxes broke loose and disappeared beneath the churning waters.

Sam struggled to keep the raft in the center of the river, dodging the boulders that appeared in their path. The raft was floating, but underwater.

Screams died in Davina's throat as the river went mad—tons of water driven berserk, making a chaos of thunder and wildness. Then, as quickly as the rapids had appeared, they ended. The raft was suddenly floating peacefully in a gentle eddy.

Awash with relief, Davina began to laugh, the sounds of her relief ringing from the canyon walls. "I can't decide whether I hated that or loved it," she gasped.

Sam grinned. "It's always that way—exhilaration, terror, followed by supreme peace. As wicked as this river is, I have to admit that it provides every emotion."

As Davina busied herself by bailing out the water that remained in the bottom of the raft, Sam examined their store of supplies.

"What did we lose?" she asked, looking up when she heard him swear softly under his breath.

"It's not all that bad," he assured her. "A few cans of beans, some tortillas, extra mosquito repellent—that's about all."

Davina didn't think such a minor loss could have generated such a pungent curse. "What else?"

His answering expression was strangely sheepish. "My cigarettes," he admitted.

She had to struggle to keep the smile from her face. "What a shame."

He laughed at that—a warm, vibrant sound that heated her to her toes. "You're a lousy liar, sweetheart. But as it turns out, I've been meaning to quit, anyway. I suppose this little accident just speeded up my decision a bit."

Reaching out, Davina curled her fingers around his. "Don't worry, Sam, you'll be far too busy to miss them."

As he lifted her hand to his lips, Sam's eyes stayed on hers. "Is that a promise?"

As she had on so many other occasions, Davina felt herself succumbing to the invitation in those tawny-gold eyes. "A promise," she whispered.

Heat kindled in his gaze. "I'll hold you to that," he murmured.

He wanted to kiss her, but didn't. Feeling the way he did at this moment, Sam wasn't at all sure he could stop with a mere kiss. And unfortunately, both the time and the place left a great deal to be desired.

"We'd better get going."

Davina's soft sigh echoed his own obvious regret. "I suppose so."

As they floated down this lazy stretch of the Usumacinta River, Davina couldn't help thinking how natural it seemed—to be there with Sam. They worked well together. And they certainly loved well. Over these past few days Davina had realized that until Sam, she had not begun to experience true passion.

It had been that passion that had made her so uneasy in the initial stages of their relationship. She certainly hadn't wanted to acknowledge the attraction she felt for him. On the contrary, she'd been fighting her feelings from the beginning, continually pointing out all the things they didn't have in common.

She had methodically cataloged all the sane, practical reasons she should avoid this man at all costs. But as she had lain alone—first at Molly's, then in the too-soft bed at the hotel in Valladolid—she had come to the startling conclusion that she was sick and tired of being sane, logical Davina Lowell.

She knew that any one of her friends or acquaintances would describe her as practical, dependable. Unexciting, she considered grimly. Even when she had finally taken a lover, the man had been as safe and predictable as their professional relationship.

When Brad had gone so far as to offer a halfhearted proposal, two years after the first faculty dinner they had attended together, Davina quickly listed all the logical, practical reasons marriage would be unsuitable for them at that point in time. She had not been at all surprised when Brad appeared vastly relieved by her matter-of-fact refusal.

The problem was, Davina had decided since arriving in the Yucatán, that Bradford Stevenson lacked the forceful inner strength of her father—of Sam. With Brad there would be no surprises, no excitement; no risks.

With her usual careful consideration, Davina had systematically weighed the pros and cons of making love with Sam, marking the items in neat columns on a mental slate. There would be problems. There were always problems.

And Sam was a man who lived only for the moment; their time together would last only as long as her stay in Yucatán.

Davina knew that to have acted on these unfamiliar feelings was far from prudent; she could be hurt when the time came to leave. But sometime during her lengthy period of introspection she had come to the conclusion that rewards without risk were meaningless.

She was brought out of her reflection by the realization that he was maneuvering the raft toward the shore. "Are we stopping?"

"I thought we'd call it a day—if you've had enough."

"I think I've had enough to last the next fifty years."

"You can always—"

"I'm not quitting," Davina broke in firmly.

This time his eyes held more admiration than frustration. "I'll say this for you, sweetheart—you're a glutton for punishment."

An hour later, Davina would have been forced to agree with him. Dusk brought hordes of mosquitos, the size of which she had never seen.

"I refuse to believe those are mosquitos," she complained, hunkered under the mosquito netting that made up the roof of their compact tent. "They're bomber squadrons, sent by the Maya living in Naj Taxim to do us in before we can find their sacred city."

Sam laughed. "They probably just figured out how tasty you are," he said, nibbling her neck. "God, you taste exactly like temptation. Warm and sweet and forbidden."

Davina allowed herself to enjoy his light caresses for a time, then turned to look up at him in the spreading dusk. "Will every day be like today?"

He didn't comment immediately, his fingers combing through her hair. "Do you want the truth?"

She wanted him to tell her that they'd put the hard part of the journey behind them; that from here on in it would be a piece of cake—child's play. That's what she wanted to hear. From his noncommittal tone, Davina realized that the truth was going to be a great deal less palatable.

She hooked her hands behind his head and pressed her mouth to his. "I don't think I do," she said, her words a soft breeze against his lips. "Not now. I've had all the reality I can handle for one day."

He pressed a trail of moist kisses down her throat, his lips lingering over her pulse beat, feeling it jump as he tasted her skin with the tip of his tongue.

"How about this?" he murmured, his own need spiraling as he felt the pounding of her blood against his mouth. "Can you handle the reality of this?"

Davina thought that by now she should know what to expect. She knew that his kisses could drive her to distraction and that when he touched her, her flesh turned to flame. She knew that he could lead her to the very brink of sanity, then lead her further still, to the place where passion, desire and need reigned supreme. She had experienced madness, tenderness, laughter with this man. But she could not have imagined either the havoc or the bliss her body was experiencing now.

"This isn't reality," she whispered.

His tongue glided over hers. "Oh, no? Then what is it?"

Perhaps it was because together they had tempted death and won. Or perhaps it was something deeper, more profound. Whatever the reason, everything in her life, everything that had gone before paled in comparison, and on some distant plane Davina was aware that nothing would ever be the same again.

"Magic," she managed to say.

She was burning for him, her need unrestrained, unreasonable. His mouth tempted; she surrendered to it. His hands, as they slid under the madras blouse to caress her breasts, offered ecstasy; she succumbed to their seductive promise. Her name, murmured over and over again, was like a sorcerer's incantation, inviting her to his mystic realm; she followed—hurriedly, hungrily.

Under the canopy of white netting, clothes disappeared as if by the wave of a wand, and when he slipped into her, she gave herself over to the heat. To the magic. To Sam.

10

As THEY SEARCHED for Naj Taxim, Sam and Davina developed a workable system. Setting up camp, they would explore the region around the area as thoroughly as the thick jungle allowed, moving downstream the following day. It was slow going; they had been at it for ten days and were already falling behind Sam's proposed schedule. As she trudged through the miles of wilderness, Davina found the jungle to be as inhospitable as it was inscrutable.

Snakes lurked in the shadows, ticks infested the vegetation, and on more than one occasion, dropping branches produced avalanches of stinging ants. Once, as she stumbled over a root overgrown with dense vines, she grasped a friendly-looking tree and the surgically sharp thorns of the innocuous-appearing escoba palm made pincushions of her hands.

That experience taught her not to trust anything at first glance. The tropical forest was such a totally hostile environment that she found it a paradox that in such surroundings the Mayan civilization had reached its zenith.

On more than one occasion, Davina felt as if she and Sam were being silently observed as they trekked through the jungle. Once she even thought she had caught a glimpse of someone who vaguely resembled the Indian who had pushed her into the Sacred Cenote at Chichén Itzá. Telling herself that these ominous feelings were only the product of an overactive imagination stimulated by their alien, treacherous surroundings, she decided not to mention them to Sam. It would only give him another argument for his attempt to convince her to turn back.

This particular morning, however, Davina could not shake the feeling that they were being watched. She could feel the eyes burning into her back, but whenever she'd turn around there would be nothing but more miles of impenetrable jungle. Still, she could not ignore the idea that this time it was more than her imagination.

"Sam," she said softly, after experiencing the uneasy feeling for more than an hour, "I think someone's following us."

Sam cut a path through a tangled vine with his machete. "Actually, it's several someones," he answered calmly.

Despite the stifling heat, Davina's blood went ice-cold. "You've known we were being followed and you didn't say anything?" she hissed, her anxious eyes darting around, seeking the silent stalkers.

"I didn't want to frighten you."

"Well, that's very considerate of you," she said dryly, accepting his hand as he helped her over a rotting tree limb. "But don't you think I deserve to know when we're in danger?"

Sam stopped in his tracks, causing Davina, who had been carefully avoiding another escoba palm, to walk right into him. She opened her mouth to complain about his sudden halt when the sight of the muscle jerking along his grimly set jaw made her mouth go dry.

"Davina," he said very quietly, his gaze directed over her head, "I'm letting you know that we're in danger."

Turning slowly around, she drew in a deep, terrified breath as she came face-to-face with the rifles a trio of grim-faced Indians were pointing in their direction.

"Oh, my God. Whatever happened to spears and obsidian tomahawks?" she murmured under her breath.

Sam's answer was short and succinct. "Progress."

There was no misunderstanding the Indians' instructions as they waved the weapons, directing Sam and Davina forward. Before they moved, however, the tallest of the three men divested Sam of his pistol.

"We're going to get out of this, Davina," Sam promised under his breath as they were marched through the jungle. "You have to trust me."

"I do," she whispered.

In truth, Davina had never trusted anyone or anything the way she had come to trust Sam McGee. She vowed that once Sam got them out of this mess, she was going to take time to seriously evaluate her feelings for him. At the moment, however, it was all she could do to keep her feet moving forward when her bones had the consistency of water.

They had not gone far when they entered a sheltered clearing. The cluster of houses—structures of wooden poles and thatch—could have been Mayan homes of antiquity. Outside one such house a woman cuddled a baby while another was busily grinding breadnuts. Across the way, a young girl was weaving an intricately designed cotton cloth. A small group of naked children played with a pair of spider monkeys, laughing delightedly at the small simians' antics. Nearby, on small earthen terraces, men tended an array of crops—corn, tomatoes, pumpkins and gourds.

As they walked through the compound, people stopped and stared unabashedly, obviously not used to intruders in their midst. Davina told herself over and over again that even here in the jungle, people were answerable to the Mexican laws. And murder was a capital offense. Of course that was only if the murderers were captured. It would be a vastly simple matter to kill two *americanos* and let the crocodiles and piranhas take care of the bodies. Who would ever know?

The sudden sound of Sam's laughter shook her from her depressing thoughts. Davina turned on him. "I'm certainly glad you've found something funny about all this."

"It's Santos Xiu," Sam explained, the relief evident in his voice. "These are his people."

"Who in the world is Santos Xiu?"

Sam pointed at the tall, regal-looking man walking toward him. "Him."

A moment later, Davina was stunned to see the two men embracing like long-lost brothers. They conversed eagerly in an Indian dialect she could not comprehend, but from the nods and approving glances thrown her way by Santos Xiu, she discerned that at least part of their conversation concerned her.

"Santos is an old friend of mine. He sent these guys out to find us," Sam explained. "We're invited to dinner."

Davina was confused. Did that mean that their captors were now their hosts? "What kind of friend uses guns to extend his invitation?"

Sam shrugged. "The jungle's a tough place; it's better to stay on your guard. But now that everything's settled, it'll be okay."

As if to confirm his statement, the elderly Indian barked an order to the guards. Sam's pistol was immediately returned.

"I think I've aged a hundred years," Davina complained as Santos led them to his home.

"Don't feel like the Lone Ranger."

Now that she was fairly well assured she was not going to die—not today, at any rate—Davina allowed herself the pleasure of looking around the small group of huts. She had the feeling she'd stumbled back in time at least a thousand years. As she turned the corner and almost walked into a large wooden cage, she gasped, instinctively clutching Sam's arm.

"What's that?"

"A jaguar."

"I know that," she complained. "I want to know what it's doing here."

Davina was forced to wait impatiently while Sam exchanged a few words with Santos. "It's for tomorrow's ceremonies," Sam said at length. "You see, Santos is an *h-men*, a priest who serves the old Mayan gods. One of his grandchildren is possessed by an evil spirit, so tomorrow they're going to sacrifice the jaguar to exorcise the spirit, then sell the jaguar pelt for a tidy profit."

Davina glanced at the silent priest. The Oriental cast of his features bespoke his Asian forebears, and his eyes, as they stared back at her, were oddly remote. But she had not missed the flicker of emotion in those dark eyes when he had answered Sam's question. The man was obviously as concerned about his grandchild as any grandfather residing in the United States would have been.

"Please tell him that I hope the child will recover," she said softly.

Sam's look was openly admiring. "You are just one surprise after the other, lady," he murmured. "I'm beginning to wonder if anything can rattle you."

Oh, you can, Sam McGee, she answered silently as he turned back to Santos, relaying her words. *Every time you look at me that way.* As Sam translated, the elderly man's smile gave Davina his appreciation for her good wishes.

They were led to a tiny house that consisted of sticks lashed together. The high thatched roof was designed to provide insulation against the oppressive heat. As they entered, Davina's sweeping gaze took in the furnishings: a water drum, two low stone benches, a low table, and in the center of the room, a firepit with a grinding mill for corn. A pair of hammocks were attached to the beams.

Waving his hand as if to invite them to make themselves at home, the elderly priest studied Davina briefly, said something to Sam, bowed formally, then left them alone.

"Santos said we should rest before the festivities," Sam translated. "His daughter will come for us in an hour or so."

"What did he say about me?"

Sam rubbed his chin. "It's a little complicated to explain."

"Try," she suggested.

"All right," Sam said with a sigh of resignation. "He also said that he was honored to meet Sam McGee's new wife."

Davina stared at him. "Wife? Where did he get that idea?"

"What did you want me to tell him—that you've hired me to find the lost city of Naj Taxim?"

Davina's chin came up a fraction. "At least that would have been the truth."

Irritation flickered in the depths of his eyes, turning them a brilliant, dangerous gold. "If I'd told Santos that, the first thing that would have happened is that he'd have laughed us both right out of here.

"Of course, a tall tale like that is too good not to spread, so before tomorrow morning, every Indian, poacher, rebel, and monkey in the jungle would have known precisely what we're doing here. Is that what you really want, Davina?"

Davina acknowledged his point with a brief nod. "I suppose you did do the right thing, after all," she said. "So what did you tell him we were doing?"

Sam grinned. "I told him we were on our honeymoon and wanted to get away from all our friends."

Davina laughed, as she was supposed to. Try as she might, she couldn't stay mad at him.

As DAVINA TOOK PART in the festivities, she couldn't help thinking how fortunate she was to be able to have such an experience. The village had maintained many of its ancestral customs, so once again she felt as if she had stepped backward in time. Even the exuberant baseball game she was encouraged to join in with Sam only echoed an ancient enthusiasm that was witnessed by ball courts in virtually every Mayan city. Like their ancestors, the modern-day Maya were passionate ball players, and more than one heated argument ensued after a questionable call.

"Thank God the losers aren't put to death these days," Sam muttered, after striking out in the bottom of the ninth inning, an act that forfeited the game to their opponents. The brief flare of ill will that had arisen during the game disintegrated as the players toasted one another's efforts.

The sense of community, of mutual interdependence, was evident among the villagers. When Davina questioned the reason for the mountain of lime at the edge of the village, the women, speaking through Sam, explained that it was easier to grind corn into meal after first soaking it in lime and water. The villagers worked together, they told her, heating chunks of limestone in order to pulverize them; and the great mound of lime was available to all.

By the time she had shared in a dinner of pork, chicken, tortillas and a thick bean soup, Davina had begun to experience a feeling of kinship with Santos Xiu's people.

"This sure beats sleeping on the ground," Sam said as he stretched out on one of the hammocks after they had returned to the house.

"You probably won't feel that way when you roll out onto the floor."

"It's not as tricky as it looks."

Dubiously, she allowed him to coax her onto the woven hammock. "It really is comfortable," she allowed.

Sam put his arm around her shoulder, drawing her against him. "I've got one back in Calderitas. Believe me, down here they're a lot cooler and more comfortable than any bed."

He brushed his lips against hers. "Not that any bed is going to stay cool too long with you in it," he added with a rakish grin.

Davina snuggled happily into his arms, and for a time they remained silent, contented simply to be together. "I like your friends," she said after a time.

"They sure liked you. Especially the kids. They were hanging on to you like a bunch of baby opossums."

Davina smiled at the memory. "I like children."

Taking care not to tilt the hammock, Sam leaned up on one elbow in order to look down into Davina's face. The moonlight streamed through the thatched roof, providing sufficient illumination for him to see the way her eyes had softened at the idea of children.

"I suppose you and your professor plan to have a few little archaeologists running around the house," he said offhandedly.

Davina was surprised at the mention of Brad. Despite the fact that she had seen her father's assistant only a little over two weeks ago, it seemed as if her relationship with Bradford Stevenson had taken place in another lifetime. She couldn't resist a slight, regretful sigh.

"Davina?" Sam brushed an errant strand of hair off her cheek. "Have I ventured into forbidden territory?"

He could feel her backing away from him emotionally and wondered why in the hell the good professor had let Davina get away. The first thing he was going to do, once they had returned to civilization, was send old Bradford Stevenson a case of the cantina's best whiskey.

Davina waited a moment to speak, trying to gather her thoughts so she could explain coherently. "No," she said quietly, "it's a logical enough question, especially at my age."

He brushed his lips against her hair. "And an ancient old age it is, too, sweetheart. My God, I don't know why I'm wasting my time with a woman of such advanced years."

She managed a smile. "To tell the truth, I don't think I would have ever married Brad, so the fact that he didn't want children is probably a moot point."

"But you did. Want children," he added.

Davina swallowed the lump in her throat. What on earth was the matter with her? She never got overly emotional, but here she was, on the verge of breaking down into tears just because she was single, childless, and her biological clock seemed to be ticking faster every day.

Taking a deep breath, she assured herself that it was only the stress of this trip. Once she returned home to Boston, her life would settle down into its comfortable if admittedly predictable routine, and she would look back in awe at the depth and range of emotions she had experienced over such a brief period of time.

"Of course I'd like children," she managed to say calmly. "I think most women would. But if it turns out that I'm not destined to be a mother, it certainly won't be the end of the world."

"Not every woman wants children," Sam corrected quietly. "Melanie sure as hell didn't."

She was surprised by the raw emotion that flashed across his moon-shadowed face. "Is that why you got a divorce?" she asked cautiously.

"When you get a divorce," Sam said slowly, carefully, "I don't think there's ever one single reason."

He knew that this was the time to tell Davina about Palmer Kirkland—to confess about his part in the Amazon disaster—but he couldn't quite force the words from his mouth. Instead, he opted for middle ground.

He leaned back, drawing her into his arms as he rested his chin on the top of her head. "I have two brothers," he began quietly. "Michael is three years older and a banker in Philadelphia; James is my younger brother—God, he must be thirty-five now," Sam said, the surprise evident in his voice. "Anyway, the last I heard, he was a financial reporter for the *Washington Post*."

"The last you heard?" Davina's voice was softly persuasive.

"I haven't exactly kept in touch."

"Oh." She waited for Sam to elaborate, but when he remained silent, she dared press a bit further. "Are your parents still alive?"

"Yeah, or at least they were five years ago. Mom was on the faculty of the Philadelphia Academy of Fine Arts and Dad had just retired when I came down here."

"Retired from what?"

"Insurance."

"He sold insurance?"

"In a way," Sam said reluctantly, wondering what had got him started on this family saga in the first place. "Actually, he owned a company. He sold it and now he's donating his time working as an industry counselor to small businesses."

Davina turned her head to stare at him. "He *owned* an insurance company? A whole company?"

Sam shrugged. "It wasn't that big a company."

"Good heavens," she breathed, "you must be very rich, Sam McGee." Now she was dying to know what he was doing down here, living the impoverished life of an expatriate American.

"My family's wealthy," he corrected.

From his grim tone, Davina wondered if Sam could possibly have been disinherited. She was about to tell him that it wouldn't matter, that it wouldn't change her feelings for him in the slightest, when he tightened his arms around her and crushed his mouth hard against hers.

There was passion in the heated kiss, but there was a fierce, unbridled desperation, as well. If talking about his family was so painful to him, Davina swore never to bring it up again. Dragging her fingers through his hair, she forgot about his parents, her father, Brad, her reasons for coming to the Yucatán. She clung to him, luxuriating in the feel of the hard male body pressed against her. Had any man's arms ever felt so right?

Tomorrow morning, Sam told himself, he'd have to begin planning again. He'd have to worry about keeping Davina safe; he'd have to prepare to handle her grief when and if they discovered proof of her father's death. And, most difficult of all, he would have to begin accepting the idea of her returning to Boston. Where she belonged. Without him.

Yes, tomorrow he would have to think of all those things. But not tonight, he decided. Not this one perfect night.

IT WAS SOMETIME in the middle of the night when Davina awoke, needing to visit the bathroom facilities a few yards from the house. Nothing about the night sounds of the jungle was very inviting, and she hated the idea of going out there alone. But she also didn't want to wake Sam. Despite her attempt to keep up with him, Davina was well aware that she was proving a burden to him on this exploration.

He set up the camp every night, did most of the cooking, was constantly cutting back vines for her, helping her over fallen trees, and of course there had been that fiasco with the escoba palm. To Davina's surprise, Sam hadn't offered a word of criticism; instead he'd patiently pulled the thorns out one at a time, covered the wounds with a thick salve, all the while offering encouraging, gentle reassurance.

Sam definitely needed his sleep, Davina decided. Besides, it was only a short run. And the villagers were certainly friendly enough. What could happen?

She was halfway to the privy when a low, threatening growl caught her attention. As she realized that she would have to pass the caged jaguar, Davina's blood ran a little colder, but she took a deep, calming breath and continued on.

She was on her way back to the little house, mentally patting herself on the back for accomplishing her solo excursion, when she came face-to-face with him: the man Sam believed tried to kill her by pushing her into the Sacred Cenote—the one she had imagined following them all this time. She opened her mouth to scream, but the threatening sight of the machete in his hand caused the scream to die in her throat.

"Who are you?" she whispered through lips that had gone suddenly dry. "What do you want?"

Those heavily hooded midnight eyes that she had not been able to dismiss entirely from her mind flashed dangerously as the silent Indian approached. His face had been painted with bold streaks of crimson and yellow that served to accentuate his high cheekbones and cruel mouth. Although he said not a word, Davina knew that Sam had been right all along. For whatever reason, this man was determined that she not reach Naj Taxim alive.

"Take one more step, and machete or no machete, I'll scream for help," she warned.

As he raised his arm, the metal blade of the weapon gleamed silver in the slanting moonlight. Davina quickly ducked out of the arc of the machete's vicious stroke before realizing that the blade had not been meant for her. With one deft slash, the Indian had cut the rope on the jaguar's slatted cage and just as quickly ripped open the door.

A pair of gleaming yellow eyes emerged from the darkened shadows as the animal instantly took advantage of the opportunity to make his escape. Not wanting to do anything to startle the jaguar, Davina covered her mouth to keep from screaming.

As the jaguar approached slowly, stealthily, Davina's initial instinct was to run. Frantically she looked around, trying to judge the distance to the nearest building. It was much too far. There seemed to be no escape. If she did try to run, the beast would give chase and be on top of her before she could make ten yards.

There was an outside chance that if she called for Sam, he could shoot it before it could get to her. But Davina didn't think the odds of that happening were much better than with the first choice.

She began cautiously backing away, inch by inch. Unfortunately the jaguar's forward progress seemed to be speeding up. "No," she whispered. "Please go away. Please."

The only response from the huge yellow cat was a continuous low growl that sounded for all the world like an amplified purr. Davina was beginning to think that she might have a chance, when she tripped on an abandoned baseball bat and fell backward onto the moist ground. The sudden movement was all the jungle cat was waiting for. He was only a few inches away when she heard Sam shout.

"Davina! Roll out of the way!" A moment later an explosion shattered the night air.

Sam cursed as the pistol jammed. Angered by the bullet now lodged in his shoulder, the jaguar spun around, his gleaming amber eyes flashing hatred as he leaped toward the unwelcome intruder. Replacing the clip, Sam managed to get a second shot off just as the cat sprang toward him, hitting him full in the chest before falling dead to the ground.

Davina stared down at the now lifeless jaguar, as if unable to believe he was really dead. Then she looked around for her attacker, not surprised to discover that once again he had melded into the black, tangled jungle. When she finally turned her grateful gaze to Sam, Davina gasped at the sight of his bloody shirt.

"Oh, my God, you're hurt!" Forgetting her earlier fright, she was on her feet in seconds.

Sam glanced down at his arm. Now that she'd mentioned it, it was beginning to hurt like hell. "It's just a scratch. His claws must've gotten me on the way down."

"You've already proved that you're a hero, Sam," Davina said as she hurriedly unbuttoned his shirt. "You don't have to be such a stoic one besides."

The gunshots had drawn a crowd, and as Sam began explaining to the excited villagers exactly what had occurred, Davina ducked into the house to get the first-aid kit. When she would have doused the long, angry gouges with antiseptic, Sam caught her hand, forestalling her nursing attempts.

"Santos sent his daughter for some herbs. They'll be fine."

She shot him a frustrated look. "Really, Sam McGee, if you think I'm going to entrust your life to some Mayan witch doctor, you've got to be crazy."

"Santos knows what he's doing," Sam insisted. "Besides, it's his village. Think what it'd do to his reputation if I refused his treatment."

She ground her teeth, furious at his damnable obstinacy. "Think what it will do to your arm if you get blood poisoning," she shot back. "Or will you then let Dr. Santos amputate it with his magic machete?"

His legs were turning to rubber. Leaning back against the wall of the house, Sam slid down to the ground. "Has anyone ever told you that you've got a sharp tongue?" Was the ground tilting or was he? Sam closed his eyes as the dizziness threatened to overcome him.

Davina pressed the wet cloth she had brought with her against his forehead. "I don't want you to die, Sam."

When he opened his eyes at that, Davina could have wept at the pain she saw in them. "I'm not wild about the idea myself, honey. But don't worry. You're stuck with me for the duration."

"Until Naj Taxim," she whispered, unaware of the tears pouring down her cheeks.

"Until Naj Taxim," he agreed, fighting back the taste in his throat. "Davina?"

She cradled his head in her lap. "Yes, Sam?"

"I think I'm going to pass out now."

With that, Sam quit fighting the inevitable and drifted off on floating waves of pain.

11

FROM THE VERY BEGINNING, Davina had scant faith in Santos's medical skills. After she'd watched him in action, any hope she had managed to cling to, for Sam's sake, had diminished. The priest began his treatment by peering into a *zaztun*, a small glass sphere that reminded Davina of a psychic's crystal ball. The glass was being used to diagnose Sam's problem, one of the villagers with a modicum of English skills explained quietly.

"I know his problem," Davina exploded. "His arm was torn open by a jaguar. He needs an antiseptic, and then we have to get him to a hospital as soon as possible!"

Her frantic words needed no translation. Santos frowned back over his shoulder, an expression echoed by the young woman who stood over Sam, swinging a censer of burning incense. The room was rapidly becoming engulfed in a bittersweet cloud of gray smoke. Santos spoke briefly to the man standing beside Davina.

"Santos assures me that your husband will recover," the villager translated. "You will see. He will sleep while the gods fight the evil spirits. There is an anthill nearby. Tomorrow morning, the first two ants who venture out will take on Sam's pain. When he wakes, the spirits and the pain will be gone."

Davina didn't believe a word of it, but Sam had insisted that she allow Santos to treat him. And even if she were to go against his wishes, the memory of those rifles kept her from interfering in what she considered a fruitless task. She watched bleakly as Santos smoothed a foul-smelling herbal solution over Sam's arm, then wrapped the wound in wet leaves.

He spent another hour chanting over the unconscious patient. After that, speaking through the translator, he instructed Davina on how to continue Sam's care throughout the night. Finally, giving her an encouraging pat on the shoulder, he departed, leaving Davina to reapply the noxious herbal mixture to Sam's arm, changing the wet leaves every half hour as instructed.

Sometime during the unbearably long night, he had struggled to sit up, his feverish, restless eyes wide open as they stared off into space.

"Where do you think you're going?" she asked, pressing her hand against his chest.

"To get a blanket. I'm so cold." He looked at her, his gaze revealing confusion. "Don't understand. It's never cold in the jungle."

"It's because you're burning up." As weak as he was, Davina's strength proved superior as she coaxed him back onto the reed pallet. "Just rest, Sam. I'll try to break your fever."

Through the interpreter, Santos had explained that the fever was a very good sign. It meant that the battle within Sam was going well. Davina was not the least bit encouraged.

For one brief, fleeting moment, his eyes cleared. "Davina? You won't leave?"

Beads of sweat glistened on the blazing skin of his forehead. Fighting back her tears, Davina pressed her lips against his brow. "I won't leave."

His hand crept along the mat to cover hers. "Thank you, Davina," he said solemnly. "This is very nice of you." His eyelids drifted shut again.

All during the night Davina continued applying the herbs to his arm. The deep gashes were still red and angry, but she had to admit that the treatment had stopped the bleeding. Between periods of administering to his arm, she attempted to soothe his feverish body with cool water from a thick stoneware jug.

But as Sam tossed and turned fitfully on the reed pallet, Davina grew more and more concerned. With the exception of that single brief interlude when he'd asked her to stay with him, it had been hours since he had shown any sign of recognizing her.

By the time the morning sky dawned pink and gold, Santos returned to the house, a broad, self-satisfied grin on his dark features. When he beckoned for Davina to follow him, she hesitantly obliged, not knowing what to expect. She had trusted him once, and as far as she could tell, Sam's condition had not improved even the slightest bit. If anything, his delirium had increased in the predawn hours; on more than one occasion he had called out her name, and for a time he had rambled on incoherently about her father.

He was out of his mind with the fever. During the long, lonely hours of her vigil, Davina had come to the conclusion that the only way Sam stood a chance would be if she could get him back to the raft so they could return to civilization, where he could receive proper medical care. As she followed Santos across the compound, Davina was wondering what her chances were of receiving his help in her mission.

At the edge of the village, Santos came to a halt in front of a tall anthill covered with thousands of dead insects. Stunned by the outrageous possibility that he could by some chance know what he was doing, Davina lifted skeptical but hopeful eyes to his friendly ones. Nodding vigorously, Santos gave her a broad, reassuring smile. Then, bowing formally as he had last evening, he left Davina to stare in awe at the anthill.

As she continued to apply the herbal medication on schedule throughout the morning, Davina allowed herself the slightest modicum of optimism. Perhaps it was only her imagination, stimulated by that strange scene at the anthill, but she thought Sam's color might have been a little better than it had been last night. He was still pale, but that frightening, unearthly gray shade was gone. And the swelling around his wound seemed to have diminished ever so slightly.

"Don't you dare die on me," she warned as she sponged him down for the umpteenth time. "I need you, Sam McGee."

And for a great many more reasons than your tracking ability, she added mentally. Somehow, when she wasn't looking, Sam McGee had become more important to her than she ever would have imagined possible.

Sam finally awoke several hours later to find Davina looking down at him with very real concern. She had been going out of her mind as she had been forced to sit by helplessly, watching him drift in and out of consciousness.

"How are you feeling?"

He managed a weak smile. "Better. Did you get the license plate number?"

She ran a cooling cloth over his dry, parched lips. "License plate?"

"Thanks. Of that truck that ran over me."

Tears of regret sprang to her misty eyes. "Oh, Sam."

"Hey," he complained, "it was supposed to be a joke. I'll admit it wasn't a very good one. But you can't expect me to be at my best, under these circumstances."

Davina appreciated Sam's attempt at levity, but she knew that were it not for her, he'd be back in his cantina in Calderitas, happily drinking his tequila and making love to willing, uncomplicated women who didn't end up getting him nearly killed.

"Oh, Sam, I'm so very, very sorry."

He reached out and took hold of her hand, twining their fingers together. "You can't let this little setback discourage you, sweetheart. And for the record, it wasn't your fault."

"Of course it was," she retorted. "If I had listened to you, we never would have been here in the first place."

"That's all water under the bridge. I just wish I could improve on my timing a little."

"What do you mean?" She brushed his damp hair off his forehead. The fever seemed to have lessened considerably.

"I keep rushing to the rescue after you've already been attacked; it'd be a nice change of pace if I got there before the crime."

Attacked. Even as Davina had nursed Sam around the clock, she had not been able to put the threats on her life out of her mind. The idea that anyone would want to kill her—a staid, proper professor of archaeology from Boston University—was both ludicrous and terrifying at the same time.

Sam had warned her that the jungle was clever at hiding its secrets. First Naj Taxim. Then her father. And now? Could her assassin be lurking in the dense tropical growth, watching her, waiting, biding his time until his next attack? And if so, why?

"I don't suppose this latest incident has changed your mind about going home?" Sam asked hopefully.

Davina shook her head slowly, regretfully. "You know I can't do that, Sam. Not until I find my father."

His head was splitting. Sam cursed softly as he pressed his hand against his temple. "I'll say this for you, sweetheart," he muttered as he closed his eyes again, "you definitely inherited the Lowell stubbornness."

Concerned as she was about Sam, Davina didn't focus on his words. She could only think how frighteningly close she had come to losing him.

Sam continued to sleep throughout the remainder of the day and all during the following night. Whenever Santos checked in on his patient, which was often, Davina's heartfelt gratitude contained a newfound esteem. Standing vigil over the sleeping man, the two individuals from such disparate cultures managed to come to a mutual respect and understanding.

To Davina's vast relief, Sam awoke the following morning with clear eyes, no pain and a ravenous appetite. Santos had blushed a coppery hue when Davina gave him an enthusiastic hug, but he appeared to appreciate the gesture. After a hearty meal of corn tortillas and beans, Sam and Davina said their goodbyes to the villagers and set out once again into the jungle.

Although Davina insisted that Sam take it easy, at least in the beginning, he refused to coddle himself—his words, not hers. He complained vociferously about the herbal ointment she made him spread on his arm three times a day as Santos had prescribed for the next week, but Davina had become a convert. Whatever the noxious stuff was, it seemed to work. Muttering about her damn hardheadedness, Sam nevertheless obliged her by grudgingly accepting the treatment.

"So where are we going today?" she asked on their fifteenth morning on the river. It had been a scorching, airless night and the day didn't hold promise of being any cooler.

Sam stretched, testing the strength of his arm. It was almost as good as new, he thought with satisfaction. For a moment there, when the jaguar had hit, he'd thought for sure he was a goner.

"I thought we'd try to get as far as Bethel and work our way outward from there."

They were halfway to Yaxchilán. If they hadn't found Naj Taxim by the time another two weeks had passed, Davina would be forced to admit her map was indeed a fraud. She watched idly as Sam picked up her shoes, opened the tent flap and shook them out. An arch-tail scorpion fell onto the ground and disappeared beneath the rotting foliage.

"Jungle survival rule number thirty-seven," he said casually. "A prudent explorer shakes his shoes out in the morning."

"I could learn to hate this place," she muttered in frustration.

Sam reached out, running his fingers through her short blond curls. During their stay in the village, Davina had given in to the inevitable and cut off her heavy braid with the compact scissors attached to Sam's ever-ready Swiss army knife. To her surprise, once the weight and length were gone, her hair had demonstrated a natural curl. She still wasn't used to the new style, but she had to admit it was several important degrees cooler.

Sensing her depression, Sam sought to bring a smile to her downcast face. "You look like a pixie this morning." His tawny eyes moved from the top of her head, over her slender body, clad in a green T-shirt and shorts, down to her feet. "A wood nymph." He rubbed his chin thoughtfully. "Peter Pan," he decided.

Davina understood what he was trying to do and appreciated the effort. But at the moment she was feeling hot, dirty and more than a little discouraged. The humidity in the air made breathing difficult, and when she did draw in a deep breath, she also inhaled the rank smell of decay as fallen limbs and dead trees rotted moistly underfoot.

"You've no idea how good that makes me feel," she muttered, lacing up her shoes after examining them thoroughly. "To be compared to an adolescent boy."

Sam fought back a smile as she marched out of the tent, intent on brushing her teeth with water from the canteen. She'd been one hell of a sport, he'd give her that. It had been quite an experience, watching the meticulously neat archaeology professor traipsing through miles of vine-choked jungle.

Even when her hands had turned into a human pincushion on that escoba palm, Davina hadn't complained. Instead, she'd muttered a particularly pungent series of oaths, before gritting her teeth as she turned to Sam for first aid. Although her cheeks went decidedly pale before it was over, she had not allowed a murmur of protest to escape her lips as he pulled the scores of stinging thorns, one at a time, out of her skin with a pair of needle-nose pliers.

Not only had she not been the slightest bit condescending to Santos and his people, she had honestly appeared to enjoy their company. She had maintained her calm during that fiasco with the jaguar, and after her fear for his survival had subsided, she had even expressed admiration for Santos's ancient medicinal skills.

All in all, Sam considered, Davina Lowell had turned out to be one delightful surprise after another. Despite the fact that the Usumacinta was an inauspicious location for a romance, with its sweltering heat, ever-present insects and inhospitable tribesmen camped along its banks, he found himself not at all eager for the expedition to end.

"Feeling better?" he asked in a bland, friendly manner when she returned to the campsite.

With her teeth cleaned, and after a sponge bath—which she knew was a waste of water but which she refused to give up—Davina did indeed feel a great deal more human. She smiled her thanks as she took the drink he handed her. Although in the beginning it had been difficult to give up her morning coffee, she had come to appreciate the *horchata*, a cooling drink made from almonds and rice.

"I'm sorry I snapped at you."

Sam cupped her hips in his hands as he drew her closer. "You had a perfect right. After all, this isn't at all what you're used to. You're hot, tired—"

"So are you." Her eyes held his as she hooked her free arm around his neck. "And you aren't yelling at me."

Sam ran a finger casually down her side. "I got all my yelling out of the way back in Calderitas."

Davina's sleep had been restless; she had awakened that morning already tired. Nights of tossing and turning on the hard ground and days of stomping through the tangled jungle had made her aware of muscles she had not even known she possessed. But she knew that her exhaustion had nothing to do with the weakness infusing itself into her bones.

"And Chichén Itzá," she said with a breathless little laugh as his palms skimmed the sides of her breasts. "You practically roared at me back there."

His tongue slid moistly down her neck, loitering at the soft hollow where her pulse skipped a beat. "You deserved it. Do you have any idea how I felt when I saw you go over the side of that damn well?"

At the time, Davina had believed Sam's reaction to be merely another display of his ill temper. Now she realized that he had felt as helpless, as suddenly bereft, as she would feel were she to lose him. As terrified as she had been the night after the jaguar's attack. That thought brought up the unhappy but inescapable fact that day by day, hour by hour, their time together was inexorably sifting away.

"I know," she said before crushing her mouth to his. "I know how you felt." Passion erupted to steamroller over desperation. "Make love with me, Sam. I need you. Now."

It did not occur to Davina that she was begging. She only knew that somehow, when she wasn't looking, Sam McGee had become the most important thing in her life. The power of her feeling for him was so strong, so all-encompassing, that it bordered on obsession.

How should he handle this? Sam wondered, even as his hands didn't hesitate to move over her, returning her almost frantic touch. He could drag her back inside the tent, where they could spend the entire day making love in this sweltering hellhole. Or he could maintain some vestige of control and continue downstream—where a cool and inviting pool waited beyond the bend of the river.

He caught her skimming hands and lifted them to his lips, where he kissed each trembling fingertip, one by one.

"It's not that I wouldn't love to take you up on your offer, sweetheart," he said, "but if I allow you to seduce me now, you'll ruin the surprise."

She lifted a delicate blond brow. "You've been nothing but one surprise after another, McGee. What makes this one so special?"

Sam decided that resisting the silent appeal of her slender body as it brushed lightly, teasingly against his was the hardest thing he'd ever done.

"You'll have to wait and see."

"Can't you give me one teensy, tiny little hint?" she murmured beguilingly, her mouth a whisper from his.

He caught her bottom lip between his teeth. "Has anyone ever told you that you could probably be arrested for the thoughts you inspire?"

"Really?" She ran her palms down his chest.

"Really." He caught her nimble fingers just as they reached his belt buckle. "In fact, a few of the more entertaining fantasies I've been having are probably illegal in forty-nine states—not to mention the District of Columbia and various territories."

Tossing back her head she laughed—a low, rich, satisfied feminine laugh. "Only forty-nine?"

"Californians are allowed to be a little kinky," he said with an easy smile, "since they wouldn't know how to be anything else."

"Good." She tugged his shirt. "Let's pretend we're in California."

Sam could feel reason slipping away. "Later," he promised, escaping her hands as he backed away.

"Spoilsport."

"Believe me, Davina, you'll thank me for this later."

Relenting, Davina returned his grin as she ran a finger down his jawline. "I'm holding you to that, McGee."

He turned his head, catching her finger between his lips. "What would you say to a pool of sparkling fresh water, fed by a cool mountain stream?"

Her eyes widened. "That's the surprise?"

Sam's answering grin confirmed it. "Is it worth waiting for?"

Davina tilted her head back, giving him a long, appraising look. Sam had never been so thoroughly mentally undressed by a woman before and was finding the experience admittedly unsettling. But rather nice, he decided. Actually, it was damn nice.

"I suppose it is," Davina admitted at length, her eyes warming with provocatively sensual lights. "But just barely."

THE RESPITE AT THE POOL was everything Sam had promised. Taking time out from their tireless search for Naj Taxim and Jordan Lowell, they frolicked in the jade-colored waters like carefree children. Later, refreshed and renewed, they made lengthy, joyous love before continuing their journey down the river.

They had been traveling for about an hour when a boatman approached them.

"What does he want?" Davina asked, after Sam and the Indian had exchanged words. For all her knowledge of native dialects, the man could have just as easily been speaking Greek.

"He's offering to guide us to some recently found ruins," Sam said.

Although Davina could not understand the boatman's words, his furtive manner came through loud and clear. "What he means is that although the archaeologists haven't found the site, the looters have had a field day," she guessed.

"I'd say that's a distinct possibility."

Davina looked from the strangely guarded, waiting man to Sam, then back again. "I suppose we should check it out."

"If you want." His tone was decidedly unenthusiastic.

"It could be Naj Taxim."

"And it could be just another plundered site."

She combed her fingers through her curly hair. "Still—"

Suppressing a look of frustration, Sam turned back to the man with a rapid string of unintelligible words. A moment later the boatman was tying up his canoe, Sam and Davina following suit as they beached their own raft.

The silent Indian led them through a maze of thick underbrush to where, almost hidden under tangled vines and guarded by limestone outcrops and giant ceiba trees, they found the tumbled walls.

"You're right," Davina said sadly. "It's a false alarm."

Sam had taken Davina's hand to assist her over a fallen tree. He squeezed her fingers in a reassuring gesture. "Now that we've come all this way, we might as well see what the guy has to offer. If nothing else, you can go back to Boston University the first archaeologist in the field of Mesoamerican culture to describe this place."

After their carefree, love-filled morning, his inadvertent reminder of Davina's imminent return to the States was decidedly depressing. She sighed a regretful little sigh, wondering why it was that life's problems never seemed to come with easy, textbook solutions.

A very strong part of her wanted to blurt out that she didn't want to return to Boston; that her place was there, with Sam. But honesty forced her to accept the fact that such a declaration would be born of a romanticism she had been unaware she believed in. Besides, she assured herself, all such a display of feminine emotion would do would be to embarrass them both.

"If these walls are all there is, I won't exactly go back a local hero," she muttered.

She had no more than spoken when they came upon a thick limestone shelf. Underneath the shelf the enormous open mouth of a cave yawned blackly over them.

"Sam!"

Her fingernails dug into his skin and her hand was ice-cold. Sam stiffened, his free hand reaching for his pistol. As his eyes narrowed dangerously, Davina realized Sam was quite prepared to use whatever means it took to keep her safe. Including killing a man. When that thought gave her scant comfort, she refused to consider it any longer. Instead, she pointed at the figure carved in the limestone. It had the face of a monster, with coiling snakes for hair, and the tongue stuck out over the mouth of the cave.

"Sam—I recognize that stela! It was described in detail in my father's text of Naj Taxim. It guards the entrance to the city!" She threw her arms around his neck. "It's the cave, Sam. The cave is the key!"

"Davina—"

"Please don't say it. I realize that you've simply been humoring me this entire trip. But Naj Taxim exists, and now I'm finally going to prove it to you."

The feeling he had experienced at the Well of Sacrifice suddenly settled back over Sam like a cold gray fog—a sense of unearthly evil that sent a chill skimming down his spine.

"We're getting out of here," he said, yanking her back toward the river. The feeling escalated when he turned around to find that the boatman had vanished.

"We can't." Davina struggled desperately to hold her ground. "Don't you see, Sam, we can't give up now. Not when we're so close."

"Goddammit!"

The oath exploded from him, sudden and harsh in the verdant solitude of the jungle. Birds screeched, a cloud of black and yellow butterflies filled the air from some unseen hiding place and somewhere the ominous roar of a jaguar added to the animals' complaints.

Unreasonably frustrated, Sam reached into his pocket for a cigarette, forgetting for a moment that he had lost them that first day on the river. Strange that he hadn't thought about smoking in all this time—until now; until forced to come face-to-face once again with Davina's blasted Lowell obstinacy.

"I thought you'd quit smoking," Davina said, taking in his futile gesture.

"You frustrate me, Davina."

She appeared to be considering that as her soft eyes grew thoughtful. Finally she nodded, accepting the accusation. "As you do me."

"This isn't a game any longer."

"I wasn't aware that it ever was." Her voice was stronger now, more assured. "How could you possibly believe that my search for my father was a game?

"What made you think that I'd put up with all this damn heat and the insects and mud if I considered it to be nothing more than a game?"

The more she thought about Sam's arrogant attitude, the angrier Davina became. Her eyes blazed, her cheeks were stained scarlet and her chest rose and fell under her T-shirt. She was furious. And more beautiful than he'd ever seen her.

"And you," she continued, lifting her chin defiantly as she jabbed a finger into his chest, "how dare you think that I consider what we've shared a game? What kind of woman do you take me for?"

"A live one. And I'd like to keep it that way."

His quiet, understated tone had its desired effect. Davina's shoulders slumped wearily. "I hate it when you make me lose my temper. I'm really a very calm, very restrained individual. Ask anyone who knows me."

"Of course you are," he said soothingly, draping an arm around her shoulders. "And once we get back to our hotel room, you can demonstrate exactly how restrained you can be."

She stiffened. "Hotel room?"

"With a warm, deep bath," he coaxed. "And sheets. Crisp, clean sheets that feel cool against your creamy skin. And ice. You can't tell me that you wouldn't like a nice, icy margarita right now."

Davina stared up at him. "You haven't heard a word I've said."

Sam's lips grazed her ear. "Of course I have. We were talking about how I make you lose control," he said huskily. "Let's go home, sweetheart, and drive each other crazy."

Shaking her head violently, Davina broke free of his light embrace. "You can do whatever you want, McGee, but I'm going into that cave."

Muttering a particularly pungent oath that had a family of squirrel monkeys chattering in heated remonstration, Sam had no choice but to yank the lantern from his backpack and follow her.

12

SLIPPING AND SLIDING, they entered the cave. Despite the fact that Sam was holding the lantern above his head, the black walls seemed to absorb the weak yellow beam of light, and when he turned a sharp corner before Davina, she experimentally lifted her hand blindly in front of her face until her index finger touched her nose. Darkness enfolded her like a shroud.

"Sam, this is eerie. I can't see a thing," she whispered in the direction where she could sense, rather than see, he was standing.

"What did you expect? There's no way the sun could shine down here."

Davina didn't like to think about being underground, experiencing for the first time a phobia of being buried alive. She brushed something away from her face, hoping desperately that it was only a stray hair. A moment later, her hand encountered something spongy on the blackened wall and she recoiled.

"Ugh. This place is like something out of Poe."

"*The Cask of Amontillado*.... 'The thousand injuries of Fortunato I had borne as best I could,'" Sam quoted. "'But when he ventured upon insult, I vowed revenge.'"

Goose bumps rose on Davina's already chilled skin as Sam's words ricocheted about her worried mind. *It's only this place*, Davina assured herself. In the Mayan view of the cosmos, the universe was a giant square of earth where men walked. At the center of the square was the Sacred Ceiba, the giant tree of life, whose limbs extended upward to the heavens and whose roots reached into the underworld.

Xibalbá, the Mayan underworld, was an evil place inhabited by brutal gods of death and sacrifice, among them the Jaguar God of the Night. Rivers of abomination, choked with the stench of blood, formed the borders of this realm of dread and terror; caves were the entrances.

It's your imagination, nothing more, Davina assured herself without a great deal of success. *That's all.*

"Bad choice, huh?" Sam murmured, sensing her discomfort.

"Don't you know anything a little cheerier?"

"From Poe?"

Davina was forestalled from suggesting he switch writers when the penetrating half-light revealed a steep, boulder-strewn slope terraced with high flagstone walls. Near the base of one of the walls was a fragment of brightly painted pottery.

"Looters." Sam's tone was scathing.

A cursory glance around showed that the archaeological pillagers had also pried some of the walls apart. Through the gaping holes, they could view rectangular cavities.

"Tombs," Davina suggested.

Sam nodded in agreement. "Which way?"

Davina glanced around, choosing her direction at random. "That way," she said, pointing toward a broad tunnel that would allow them to continue in a standing position.

Sam checked his compass. It wouldn't do for them to get lost; some of these caves went on for miles, underground labyrinths of limestone.

"East it is."

After several twists and turns they came to a wall covered with hieroglyphics. Davina stared in awe at the elegant glyphs left behind by some ancient artist. She could almost imagine the glow of Sam's lantern to be the flickering light of the scribe's ocote pine torch. In her mind's eye she envisioned the Mayan artist, wielding his animal-hair brush with delicate, precise strokes as he carefully recorded his message for posterity.

"There are some names," she murmured, peering closely at the glyph. "And a date."

Davina struggled to decode the complicated calendar, based on a continuous procession of gods who marched along an eternal trail that had no beginning and no end.

"Sam," she said excitedly, "it's dated after Guerrero's fatal battle."

His voice counseled restraint. "That doesn't prove anything, Davina."

"I know." She ran her finger over a painting of a seated figure holding a ritual bloodletting instrument. "But you have to admit it's interesting."

"It's a lot more than interesting," Sam said in an undertone. "Congratulations, sweetheart. I think you've stumbled across a fifteenth-century predecessor of *Playboy* magazine."

Her curiosity piqued by the laughter in his tone, Davina left off her study of a panel depicting some ancient battle and turned to the piece of wall Sam indicated.

"Oh, my...Well, yes....This is highly unusual, you know," she murmured distractedly as she stared up at the vividly detailed drawings.

Sam cocked his head in an attempt to gain a new perspective on what appeared to be an orgy in progress. "Not only unusual, but highly uncomfortable. Did any of your studies ever reveal these people to be contortionists?"

Davina's eyes narrowed in speculation as she took in the particular amorous couple Sam was studying so intently. "Not at all; the Maya were normally quite decorous."

"So I see." Sam handed her the compact camera from the backpack. "You're going to be a real hit on campus when you return home with these dirty Mayan postcards, Professor."

Fighting her own answering smile, Davina ignored his teasing tone. "I'm taking these photos for posterity," she insisted firmly. "Erotica was extremely rare in Mayan art; this wall will make an extremely interesting paper."

In the beginning Sam had become irritated whenever Davina slipped into this stiff, professional behavior, but he now found the facade fascinating. The contrast between the proper Bostonian professor and wildly wanton witch was not only delightful but highly arousing, as well. He bent down to nibble provocatively on her ear.

"I'll warn you right now that your dirty paper will probably be banned in Boston."

"Sam!" Davina jumped as his teeth closed on her earlobe. "You're supposed to be holding the lantern up for extra light. This camera flash isn't all that strong."

His lips moved down her neck, but he did as she requested. "Can I help it if this stuff turns me on?"

"Everything turns you on," she muttered, trying out a different f-stop as she sought to illuminate the wall as much as possible.

He ran his free hand from her shoulder to her hip. "Complaining?"

Davina could feel something inside her coming to life. Warm, insistent. Familiar. He could make her want him so easily, she thought with an inward sigh. Still, it appeared to work both ways. Despite an admittedly rocky beginning, from the start there had been no ambivalence between them.

"Not at all," she answered, "and as soon as we get to Naj Taxim, I'll show you exactly how you make me feel."

"I'm holding you to that, sweetheart,"

Approximately ten minutes after they had resumed their exploration of the cave, they came to a fork in the tunnel.

"Which way?" Sam asked.

Davina's decision was based solely on whim. "Right," she said. "No, left." She shook her head. "Right," she reconfirmed.

"It'd probably help if you could make up your mind."

She crossed her fingers behind her back. "Definitely right."

Sam shrugged. "You're the boss."

After more twists and turns, the underground tube came to a dead end.

Sam's skeptical gaze raked the walls adorned with drawings depicting a legendary ball game pitting men and gods in a life-and-death contest. One noble player was seated on the sidelines, taking an everlasting time-out from the brutal game.

"Where to now? Straight up?"

Davina ran her hands over the solid stone wall, forcing herself not to be distracted by the art. She was momentarily saddened at the vandalism marring the torso of one of the players. It seemed that every increase in Mayan knowledge was matched by a commensurate loss.

A moment later her fingers located the dark crack. "I've found a hidden crawlway," she said excitedly.

"A crawlway?"

She tried to overcome the refusal she could hear in Sam's voice. "We've already come this far," she coaxed prettily.

"I thought I was supposed to be a guide," he grumbled. "All right," he agreed with obvious reluctance when she didn't immediately back down. "But I'm going first."

Davina was not about to argue that point.

The ceiling of the crawlway was no more than eighteen inches over their heads, and as they crept on their stomachs over the rough, damp terrain, their clothes growing wetter by the inch, Davina was beginning to doubt her own intuition. Sam had probably been right all along: it was nothing but a wild-goose chase.

Although Sam held the lantern in front of him as he shimmied along the floor of the tube, the low ceiling didn't allow for effective diffusion of light.

"Hey! Wait until you see this!"

A moment after his voice echoed through the cave, bouncing against the damp limestone walls, he disappeared from view. In her eagerness, Davina rose abruptly, hitting her head on a stalactite.

"Ouch!" she exclaimed, followed by a more heartfelt "Damn!" Stars swam on a background of black velvet behind her eyes. Even her teeth hurt, and she could still hear the resounding *clunk* ringing in her ears.

"You okay?" Sam asked.

"Sure. I've always wanted to be a couple of inches taller." Davina rubbed the lump that was rapidly building on her scalp. "Actually, I'm more mad at myself for doing such a dumb thing than I am hurt."

Her voice trailed off as her gaze circled the huge chamber. The ceiling rose at least twenty feet over their heads, and a fringed curtain of white stone hung from the distant ceiling. The sparkling dome resembled a blackened sky lit with countless twinkling stars, the brilliant illusion created by droplets of moisture decorating the tips of the stalactites. Three high walls rimmed a clear, calcite pond, and as Sam moved the lantern in a wide arc, the muted yellow glow revealed the frescoes.

The brilliant paintings were magnificent, and could be considered unrivaled among Mayan archaeological finds.

In rich reds, yellows and a particular pastel shade known as Mayan blue, artists had portrayed life among Mayan elite. One series of paintings depicted a raid against another Mayan community, from the battle to the final ritual sacrifice, the scenes so realistic that Davina could easily envision the warriors as they appeared over the hill with the first rays of rising sun.

She could hear their shouts and war cries filling the air as they displayed their banners. She could see them advance in columns down the hill to the edge of the river. The clash was horrible, the screams and shouts deafening. A din of flutes, drums and conch-shell trumpets resounded as the chiefs vainly sought to save themselves by divine magic.

"Davina?"

Belatedly she realized Sam had asked her a question. Shaking her head to clear it of the brutal battle scene, she turned toward him. Her emotions were in as much turmoil as her thoughts.

"Sorry. My mind was wandering again."

He managed a smile. "No small wonder."

Her eyes roamed the walls. "It's magnificent, isn't it?" she murmured.

"It's definitely that." His gaze dropped to the crystal pool at their feet. "It's also the end of the road."

Davina couldn't accept that idea. These walls were the most detailed recording of Mayan life that she had seen or read of. From the various artistic styles, she could tell that three, perhaps four scribes had worked hard and long on the project. They would not have dedicated such intensive labor to this cavern were it not terribly important. Her disbelieving eyes swept over the intricate figures and hieroglyphics until she found what she was searching for.

"Sam, look at that."

Alerted by her trembling tone, Sam's eyes obediently moved to the far wall. There, attired in full battle regalia, wearing an elaborately feathered headdress, was the god king of this particular group of people. He was in the bow of a canoe, his finger pointing imperiously forward.

"We follow him," she decided. "That's what all this is about. He's leading me to my father, Sam. I know he is."

Unfortunately Sam was beginning to come to the same conclusion. He also didn't like their chances. They were too much at risk in this isolated cave.

"This is too damn dangerous," he said voicing his thoughts.

But Davina had come too far to quit now. "If you want to go back, go. I'm going to find my father."

"You damned idiot!" He grabbed her arm. "Don't you realize that someone's been trying to kill you?"

"That's your opinion."

His fingers tightened. "It's a fact! Just like it's a fact that we're like ducks in a shooting gallery in here! Why in the hell can't you see that this could be a trap?" He was shouting now, and his furious words bounced off the walls of the cavern.

"This is my father we're talking about!" Her own exasperated tone matched his decibel for decibel. Somewhere deep in the dark recesses of the cave a flurry of bats flapped their wings, their sleep disturbed. "I love him! Can't you understand that?"

"Understand?" His look was incredulous. "Understand?" he repeated harshly. "Why do you think I'm trying my best to keep you alive?" He didn't give her a chance to respond. "Because I love you, dammit!"

Bewildered by Sam's gritty admission, Davina stared up at him. "You certainly don't sound very pleased about it," she said at length.

His hard, amber eyes didn't leave hers. "It was not having a choice that I found difficult to accept."

Davina considered that. "And you're a man used to your own choices; making your own way."

"Yes."

Sam's mouth was dry; his heart was pounding. In all his forty years he had only ever told one other woman that he loved her, and that had been more out of a sense of obligation than emotion. He didn't know how he had expected Davina to react, but he would have preferred anything to this slow, thoughtful scrutiny.

He hadn't meant to tell her—not now, not this way. When he had allowed himself to entertain thoughts of admitting his feelings to Davina, he had imagined a candlelight dinner, strolling musicians, the scent of tropical flowers perfuming the night air. But nothing concerning Davina Lowell had gone as planned. Why should he expect this, the most important moment in his life, to be any different?

"You've put me in a difficult position, Sam."

He lifted a brow, not trusting his voice.

"If I were to tell you that I love you now, when I'm going to do my best to change your mind about turning back, how could I know that you'll believe me? Couldn't you think I was taking advantage of the situation in order to manipulate things to my liking?"

Davina prided herself on her ability to maintain a reasonably steady voice while inside she was being battered with a multitude of complex emotions.

How like her to swing from unbridled impetuousness to thoughtful, judicious study. "Would you do that?" he asked, attempting to match her even tone.

Her eyes were intense, belying her calm demeanor. "Never."

"I didn't think so." He smiled as he held out his arms. "So come change my mind."

She clung to him, this man she loved, drawing from his strength, luxuriating in the feel of his arms around her, his lips pressing against her hair, the knowledge that somehow, in the midst of this harsh, hostile environment, love had miraculously bloomed.

She tilted her head back, her smile wobbling slightly as she fought back the tears that threatened. "I love you, McGee."

"Now, that," he said with a husky, relieved laugh, "was definitely worth waiting for."

He pressed his lips against her temple, and she sighed. His mouth took a slow leisurely journey down her face, loitering at her eyelids, her nose, her cheekbones; a low sound escaped her throat. He slipped his tongue between her teeth and she trembled.

"Sam."

His lips covered hers. "Shh," he whispered against her mouth. "Just give me one minute to convince myself this is real." He touched her tenderly, warming her skin through her clothes, his talented, clever hands coaxing her into complacency.

It could have been a minute, an hour or an eternity. But all too soon, Sam broke the blissful contact of their lips to look down at her.

"There's nothing I can say to change your mind, is there?" he asked in a low, accepting tone.

Davina posed her answer in the only way possible. "If I were missing, would you just give up on me? Would you turn back because of a little water? Or a few random accidents?"

"They weren't accidents."

"You haven't proved that. So far it's only your own personal theory." She met his frustrated gaze with feigned calm. "Would you search for me or not?"

"Dammit, Davina, that's different. You're different. And if you can't see that—"

She pressed her hand hurriedly, desperately, against his mouth, forestalling his planned argument. "I love my father," she said quietly. "Not in the same way I love you, Sam. But I do love him. And I can't just give up now—not when I'm so close."

His fingers tightened on her waist. "I don't want to lose you." His voice was rough, worry stamped on his dark features. Was ever a woman loved so, Davina wondered.

She went up on her toes, and her lips brushed his in a feathery kiss. "You won't lose me, Sam. I promise."

Knowing he was about to make the biggest mistake of his life, Sam could think of no way to avoid the consequences. It was obvious that there was nothing he could say to change Davina's mind. He was also not going to let her disappear into the bowels of this Mayan hell without him.

"Which way?" he asked wearily.

The answering light in her eyes could have illuminated the entire cave all by itself. "This way."

Unable to do anything else, Sam reluctantly joined Davina. Hand in hand they waded into the pool of crystal-clear water, following the outstretched hand of the Mayan god-king.

At the far edge of the pond, they found round holes in one of the limestone slabs. Moving it aside, Sam located a secret passage. Exchanging a long look, they entered.

Shadowy stucco figures with elaborate feathered headdresses stood solemnly along the walls, as if silently guarding the passage. A dancer held writhing serpents and a seated ruler stared ponderingly into an obsidian mirror.

Was he looking into the future, Davina wondered—when others, first her father, then she and Sam, would enter these hallowed halls? The lantern light made flickering shadows on the limestone walls, creating the illusion that the figures were animated, moving jerkily like an early motion picture.

They descended a series of steep steps, going deeper and deeper into the earth, the brilliantly engineered corbeled vaults bringing to mind the nave of a medieval cathedral. Down and down they went, twisting and turning, the passage glistening with moisture. The silence was ominous, overwhelming in its enormity as they continued their descent into what was clearly the dreaded *Xibalbá*, the Mayan underworld.

"Look," Davina whispered, pointing at a fissure in the limestone floor—like cracked ice on a frozen river.

"Probably an earthquake."

He could hear the tremor in her voice. "I certainly wouldn't want to be down here when an earthquake struck."

He didn't answer as they stepped over the split in the earth and continued on. Sam's personal opinion was that he didn't like being down there, period—earthquake or no earthquake. He had never considered himself an overly cautious man, yet this smacked of sheer folly, whichever way he looked at it.

Just when Sam was about to put his foot down and insist they turn back, they took one more sharp turn and suddenly found themselves in daylight, facing a steep, slick bank. They climbed up the bank, slipping and sliding backward one step for every three they progressed, but eventually they found themselves at the top of a small knoll. Stunned, they stared down at the scene before them.

Beyond an earthen wall was a series of glistening white temples, clasped in the green embrace of a fecund forest. In the center of the compound, laborers were cementing together stone walls, while masons faced the exterior walls with fine-cut limestone.

Davina grasped Sam's arm. "You don't think...?"

"I believe," he said slowly, deliberately, "that you've just discovered the lost city of Naj Taxim."

Despite the fact that she had never lost hope of Naj Taxim's existence, to be looking down at the fabled city was overwhelming. Her wide turquoise eyes swept the city eagerly, trying to drink everything in at once. Davina felt as if the world had somehow spun backward on its axis, allowing her to view life as it once was.

"Now what?" Sam inquired quietly.

"I don't know," Davina admitted. "We probably shouldn't just walk right in."

"Why not?" they heard a deep voice ask. "That's what I did."

At the wonderfully familiar voice, Davina spun around. Although she had consistently refused to give up hope all these long, lonely months, although she had always believed that she would locate her father alive, the sight of him standing there, only a few feet away, was almost more than she could bear.

She felt Sam's strong arms steadying her as she momentarily sagged against him. Seconds later her spinning head had cleared and she was running toward Jordan Lowell, her arms outstretched.

"Oh, Daddy," she whispered as she flung her arms around his neck. "I knew you were alive!" Her eyes were awash with tears.

"What in the blue blazes are you doing here, Davina?" Jordan Lowell asked gruffly as he stiffly embraced his daughter.

Davina clung to her father, refusing to be disturbed by his rough tone. She'd learned years ago that her father found emotional displays highly discomforting, but after all she had been through, she was determined to allow herself this one gloriously heightened moment before donning the mask of the cool, calm, collected daughter he had always preferred.

She tilted her head back to look up at him, continuing to run her palms up and down his back, needing to prove for herself that he was a flesh-and-blood man—and not merely the memory she had struggled to keep alive this past fifteen months.

"I came to rescue you."

Jordan arched a silvery brow. "Rescue me?"

"I knew you'd found Naj Taxim," she said, cupping his weathered face between her palms. Although a faint voice in the back of her mind pointed out that he looked older, less rugged, Davina ignored it, choosing instead to find him unchanged. It was all she could do not to cover that wonderfully familiar face with kisses. She refrained, knowing her father would hate such a display of unrestrained emotion.

"I knew it," she repeated forcefully. "But I was afraid you were being held captive, so I tracked down a map and came here to bring you back to Boston with me."

Her eyes were brimming with love. "Everyone else thinks you're dead," she told him, her voice choked with emotions too complicated to catalog easily.

Anger and resentment toward those doubting Thomases who had refused to believe her, worry and fear for her father's safety, relief at finding him unharmed and unequivocal love were only a few of the more easily identifiable ones.

"Your colleagues, the authorities, even Brad," she continued, spitting out her former lover's name as if it had a bad taste. "But I never believed it. I knew we'd find you!"

The tall, silver-haired man sighed wearily as he put Davina a little away from him. "I had no doubts that the story of my death would be universally accepted. My God, Davina, it never occurred to me that you wouldn't do likewise."

"I love you," Davina said simply. As Jordan's words slowly sank in, she stared at him. "What do you mean, the story of your death?" she asked in a faint whisper.

Her father scrubbed his hand over his face. When he took it away, his turquoise eyes—duplicates of Davina's—were strangely bleak. "You have to believe me when I say that I care for you, too, Davina. Very much."

She pressed her hand against the building pain in her chest, as if the gesture could stop her heart from breaking. When she finally took a breath, it was a shaky one. "But?"

His lips were a grim, unyielding line. "But I had my own reasons for wanting everyone, including you, to believe that I'd perished on my final expedition."

She crumbled so quickly that she would have fallen to the ground if Sam had not stepped forward to catch her. Holding her against him, he murmured soft, reassuring sounds against her hair. His eyes, as they lifted to Jordan's and held, burned with unmistakable fury.

At the sight of his only daughter locked in Sam McGee's clearly protective arms, Jordan cleared his throat. "Hello, Samuel."

His tone was amazingly casual, as if he found nothing at all strange about running into his former colleague deep in the middle of the Central American jungle. "I suppose I have you to thank for keeping my daughter safe."

Despite her distress concerning her father's subterfuge, despite the pain that knowledge had brought, Davina was stunned to realize that the two men were obviously acquainted. Why hadn't Sam told her he knew her father?

Sam had remained silent as Davina greeted her father, dreading what he knew was yet to come. He would give everything he owned in the world, including the deed to that beachfront property on the Islas Mujeres he'd bought five years ago, if only he could stop Jordan from revealing what he himself should have told Davina long before this. But there had never been what seemed an appropriate time. Now it was too late.

"How do you know Sam?" Davina lifted her head to ask the question Sam had been dreading.

Jordan's puzzled gaze moved from Davina's curious face to Sam's grimly set one and back again. "Hasn't he told you?"

Davina could feel the energy emanating from Sam's rigid body. Anxiety? Fear? she wondered incredulously.

"Told me what?" She could not think of anything her father could possibly tell her that would change the way she felt about Sam McGee.

"That we've worked together. Sam was Palmer Kirkland's right-hand man," Jordan divulged. "Not to mention being the bastard's son-in-law."

Davina felt her blood turn to ice. She covered her face with both hands, unwilling to look at either man. She refused to allow them to see the naked anguish she knew must be written over her features. She stood there, allowing this final act of pain and betrayal to seep through her, filling every pore, clouding her brain, weakening her body.

Then, as she forced herself to remember everything she had learned about this man during their time together, she felt it flow out of her, leaving her mind clear, her resolve strong.

Davina dropped her hands to her sides as she turned to Sam, her eyes searching deeply into his. "You told me that you're not married any longer."

"I'm not."

"And Kirkland—do you still work for him?"

"No. I haven't for five years."

Davina nodded soberly. "Since that horrid business with the Peixotos," she murmured, more to herself than to Sam. She looked into Sam's eyes and believed what she saw. "You weren't responsible."

"Of course he wasn't," Jordan agreed instantly. "Hell, Samuel fought Kirkland harder than anyone. Even at the cost of his marriage. But the man's a megalomaniac who only knows value in a profit. You can't argue with him on moral grounds—because he doesn't have any."

"I funded the expedition," Sam argued. "I was responsible for the outcome."

Jordan studied the younger man for a long, silent time. "Your efforts contributed to the discovery of the tribe, yes. But as for the outcome..." He lifted his shoulders in a weary shrug. "You did what you could, Sam. In the end, that's all any of us can do."

"I always figured you blamed me," Sam said in a low voice. "God knows, I blamed myself." His eyes, as he turned to Davina, had a strangely guarded look.

"When you brought the subject up at dinner in Valladolid, I was afraid you'd hate me if you knew the truth. That's why I kept putting off telling you."

Her gaze didn't leave Sam's stony face. "I know you, Sam. That's all I need to know."

A warming mix of gratitude and love flooded into his golden eyes. "What did I ever do to deserve you?" Sam asked wonderingly.

Despite the gravity of the situation, Davina managed a slight smile. "Some people are just lucky, I guess."

She turned back to her father. "Why did you let everyone believe that you were dead?" she asked in a soft, wounded voice.

"It's not that far from the truth," he answered quietly. "I am going to die. I've got three months, six at the outside."

Davina gasped, and Sam felt her stiffen under his arm. "No," she whispered. As both men watched, she managed to find a remarkable control from her vast store of inner strength.

"We'll take you back to Boston," she insisted firmly. "We'll bring in the very best doctors from all over the country. You'll see, everything will be all right. It has to be." It was obvious to Sam that Davina was as desperate to convince herself as she was her father.

He tightened his arm around her as Jordan regretfully shook his head. "I submitted to being poked and prodded by specialists all over the country before I left, Davina. And the verdict was unanimous: there's nothing they can do."

"But—"

"Dying is a perfectly natural life-cycle stage, Daughter," Jordan insisted. "Actually, from the moment I found out, I was trying to think of a way to spare you the burden of sitting helplessly by while I left this planet. When I learned of the map's existence, it seemed as if I'd been miraculously handed a logical solution.

"I could find the city and spend the rest of the short time I have left learning everything I could about these people. Or I could die somewhere out there in the jungle. Either alternative was far more appealing than wasting away in some hospital bed, watching you suffer more each day as modern science dragged out the inevitable process of dying."

Davina's tear-filled eyes shot angry sparks. She welcomed the anger, finding it worlds more bearable than the pain. "You wanted to spare me? Damn you! What right did you have to make such a decision on your own? Don't you think I've been going crazy, worrying about you all these months? Spare me?"

She wanted to pound her fists against his chest until he was hurting as badly as she was at this moment. She hated him for remaining calm while she was not. "You're my father! Of course I would have wanted to be with you."

Jordan maintained his collected demeanor during her outburst, eyeing her with solemn interest. "Do you know, Davina, dear," he said finally, gently, when she stopped to drink in great gulps of air, "there are times you resemble your mother so strongly I find it difficult to remember that she's actually been gone all these years. She, too, was a beautiful, passionate woman."

He shook his head. "God, how I miss her," he said under his breath, turning away so Sam and Davina couldn't view the suspicious moisture suddenly brimming in his eyes.

When he turned back, his voice was steadier, his gaze clear. "Unfortunately I tire easily these days, and to be perfectly honest, this reunion has been rather stressful, I'm afraid, for all of us. If you and Samuel don't mind, I'll take you to my quarters. You can wash up while I take a brief nap before briefing the chief on your arrival. Then tonight, over dinner, I'll introduce you to these marvelous people."

13

As THEY WALKED across the compound, they drew several interested stares, but Davina suspected it was her father's presence that allowed them to move unmolested. She was still having a hard time believing that her father had been safe all this time.

Still more incredible to her was the fact that he'd purposely misled not only his friends and colleagues but his daughter, as well. Although it was disturbing to discover that her father was not the paragon she had always thought him to be, if there was anything that this time with Sam had taught her, it was that people didn't belong on pedestals.

Before long they reached a two-story building in the central acropolis. Above the doorway a stucco head of the jaguar god proclaimed divine protection for all those who dwelt within.

"I live with the leader of these people," Jordan explained. "Sun Jaguar." As Davina hesitated in the doorway, he gave her an encouraging smile. "Don't worry, you'll be perfectly safe."

The walls of the home were made of facing stone, slanted toward each other in a way that formed a corbeled vault, a hallmark of the Classic Maya. A huge bird mask of papier-mâché and feathers hung on one of the walls, next to a spotted jaguar skin. As they entered, a woman, whom Jordan explained to be a servant, stared openly at Davina.

"It's your eyes," he explained. "You'll have to be prepared for a few startled reactions; they're exactly the color of *yax*."

Yax: the center of the universe. The blue-green color of jade, water, new corn—all the things the Maya held sacred. They were also the same shade as Jordan Lowell's eyes. Davina began to understand why her father had been granted admission to his secret society.

A moment later two other men entered the room, followed by what appeared to be an armed contingent of royal guards. Davina's blood turned cold.

"Oh, my God," she whispered, staring at the all-too-familiar grim-faced Indian with the midnight-black eyes.

Her hand had turned to ice in his. Following her gaze, Sam squeezed her fingers reassuringly. "I take it that's him?"

As her eyes locked on to the harsh face of the man who had tried to kill her not once but twice Davina could only nod.

Sam's free hand moved instinctively to the pistol in his belt. It was all he could do not to shoot the bastard where he stood.

Davina, feeling Sam go rigid beside her, risked a glance upward at his face. His eyes burned with a brilliant flame. "Please don't," she whispered desperately. "Look at them, Sam; you'd never get away alive."

Sam barely heard her. All his attention, all his emotion, was riveted on the face of the man who, because of his attacks on Davina, had become his sworn enemy. After he had survived the jaguar assault Sam had vowed that if he ever came face-to-face with this man, he'd kill him. Coldly, deliberately. He had allowed a steely, bitter anger to simmer inside himself, keeping his resolve alive, his determination strong.

But now, as much as he wanted revenge, he couldn't quite make his hand pull the pistol from his belt. Sam wondered

if the man he'd been only weeks before would have been
capable of murder and decided that he possibly might have
been. But now, as his dangerous eyes locked with the challenging dark ones of the Indian, he knew that such an act,
though it might provide a certain visceral satisfaction,
would solve nothing—except, perhaps, to put Davina in
even graver danger.

Continuing to hold the attempted assassin's gaze with the
strength of his will, Sam slowly, deliberately, dropped his
hand to his side.

"Thank God," Davina breathed, closing her eyes for a
long, thoughtful moment. "Oh, thank God."

The brief exchange had been fraught with electricity, and
even Jordan, poor as he was at reading human emotions,
could not have missed either the stark fear stamped on his
daughter's face or the fury that had come over Sam's features.

"Sam," he asked quietly, "what's wrong?"

In a few taut words, Sam explained about the attempts
on Davina's life. To her father's credit, Jordan blanched
visibly when Sam got to the jaguar story. Then, his turquoise eyes flashing with an anger every bit as intense as
Sam's when he found himself confronted with Davina's attacker, Jordan turned toward the man whose headdress revealed him to be the Sun Jaguar chief.

Jordan and the chief exchanged a few words before the
latter turned to his companion. Neither Sam nor Davina
could understand the following exchange, but to their
amazement, Davina's attacker seemed to visibly shrink in
stature as he was given what could only be a severe tongue-
lashing. Moments later the two men left the room, followed by the contingent of guards.

"The man who attacked you is an overly zealous priest,
intent on protecting the people from intruders," Jordan ex-

plained at length. The protective parent warred with the remote scientist in his strangely tremulous voice.

"You see, being hidden away in this volcanic valley, the people are safe from what the priests consider corruption from the outside world. Only a few of the high priests are allowed to leave from time to time to trade for essential goods that they can't produce themselves. This is how one of them discovered that you'd been asking around about the city. When he learned you had gained access to a map, he felt he had no choice but to stop you from reaching the city."

"He killed Davina's map salesman, didn't he?" Sam asked, knowing the answer beforehand.

Jordan nodded. "I'm afraid so." He patted his daughter's shoulder reassuringly. "I've been assured by the king that the villain will be punished for his attempts on your life, my dear. Sun Jaguar asked me to relay his deepest apologies."

Before Davina could respond, Jordan crossed the room, reaching into a chest to take out a stack of journals. "For you to read," he said, handing them to Davina. "They'll explain a great deal about my work here. Hopefully they will even manage to give both of you an insight into your attacker's misguided but somewhat noble intentions."

He rubbed his chin as he looked down at Davina thoughtfully. "Actually, my dear, now that I reconsider, your unexpected arrival may prove to be highly fortuitous—if you'd be willing to grant a dying old man a favor."

"Anything," Davina agreed fervently.

Jordan ran his fingers over the leather binding of one of the journals. "If you could take these back to Boston with you and compile the data into a record of my time here, I will go to my grave with the assurance that my life has had some meaning."

He smiled suddenly. "You'd also be helping me prove to all those closed-minded idiots that make up our profession that I was correct about the existence of this city."

Davina's fingers tightened on the diaries. "You'd trust me with your work?" she asked in a whisper.

Jordan regarded her with obvious surprise. "Of course I would, Davina. I've always admired your Aztec dissertation; your writing style is far more lively than what's usually found in our profession. I have no doubt you'll do a similar sterling job when writing about these people."

"You never said anything."

"I didn't?" Jordan blinked slowly. When he opened his eyes, they were filled with regret. "No," he said slowly, gruffly, "I suppose I didn't. I've never been very good at personal relationships, especially with people I care deeply for. I suppose that's why I became interested in archaeology; the people I deal with are usually extinct."

Dragging his fingers through his pewter hair, he took a deep breath. "I'm very proud of you," he told Davina, his deep voice quavering uncharacteristically. "You've no idea how many times I wished that your mother could have lived to see what a beautiful, talented woman you've become."

He opened his arms. "I'm sorry that I haven't told you before, but I do love you, Davina Lowell."

"Oh, Daddy." Davina could feel the tears pouring down her cheeks as she surrendered to her father's embrace. She had waited all her life to hear those three simple words, and now that she had, they sounded even sweeter than she had imagined.

After a time, Sam cleared his throat. "I hate to throw cold water on this reunion, Jordan, but what about these people? When the word gets out that Naj Taxim actually exists, the city will be overrun with people. You'll be risking another Peixotos incident."

"You and Davina will simply have to work out an agreement with the government to protect them," Jordan answered, as if he possessed not a single doubt that the pair would be up to the task.

"And by the way, dear," he surprised Davina by adding, "you've no idea how pleased I am to see you here with Sam. I never did believe that Stevenson was man enough to make you happy."

After instructing the servant women to prepare baths for both Sam and Davina, Jordan left the room. Comparing this thin, drawn man with her hardy, larger-than-life father made Davina feel as if her heart was breaking.

For the first time in her life she had glimpsed beyond the mask and witnessed the man behind the legend.

HAD IT NOT BEEN for the fact of her father's terminal illness, Davina might have enjoyed the ministrations of a pair of eager house-servants. The young women bathed her in warm, scented water, applied fragrant oil to her skin and lined her eyes with a dark kohl, much like that used by the Egyptian women of ancient times.

They appeared puzzled by Davina's short blond hair, chattering excitedly as they ran a shell comb through her thick curls. After drying her with soft linens, they wrapped her in a rainbow-hued woven cotton gown. Then they led her to a private room where Sam, also bathed, and clad in cotton trousers and shirt, was waiting for her. His tawny eyes, as they drank in the sight of her, paid compliments.

"Wow. You are one very exotic lady."

Davina lifted her gaze to a shell-framed wall mirror. "I suppose it is an improvement over Peter Pan."

He spanned the distance between them and framed her face in his palms. "I didn't mean that." His expression was as solemn as she had ever seen it. "You'll always be beautiful to me, Davina, however you wear your hair, whatever clothes you're wearing—" and there his gaze turned momentarily devilish "—or not wearing."

He bent his head, brushing his lips against hers. "It's the lady inside that pretty package that I fell in love with. And don't you ever forget it."

"How could I?" she murmured, stunned by the warmth in his golden eyes.

He nodded, satisfied. "That's better."

They fell silent for a time as they settled down on the grass mats covering the floor, neither seeming willing to be the one to initiate the conversation they both knew must come. After several long minutes, Davina softly broke the silence.

"Sam?"

He squeezed her fingers reassuringly. "I know. You're going to stay."

Her eyes revealed how difficult the decision had been to come by. "I don't have any choice."

He reached out a finger, brushing away the single tear that glistened like a diamond on her cheek. "I know."

She closed her eyes against the onslaught of emotions Sam's simple caress provoked. "All my life I've struggled to gain my father's approval, his respect," she said quietly.

"But most of all his love," Sam guessed.

Davina nodded. "I never had any friends my own age; I spent all my free hours after school in the library, searching for subjects my father might be willing to discuss with me over the dinner table."

She sighed. "While all the other kids were devouring Nancy Drew mysteries, I was wading my way through Darwin. When the other girls spent Friday nights learning the latest dance steps, I was learning to unlock ancient secrets with radiocarbon dating.

"And when those same girls were spending Saturday afternoons downtown, trying on dress after dress in search of the perfect outfit to wear on an all-important weekend date, I was at home with a textbook portraying the hunting and gathering practices of a remote Amazon tribe."

"Indubitably that thick, scholarly tome would have been authored by Jordan Lowell, Ph.D."

Davina managed a crooked smile. "Of course." She shook her head. "So many years," she murmured. "So much time wasted."

He squeezed her shoulder. "Hey, not exactly wasted. Or are you going to try to tell me that you hate your work?"

"Of course I love it, but—"

"And as for earning your father's respect, do you think he'd hand over his precious journals if he didn't think you were the best person for the job?"

"No, but—"

"And as for loving you, sweetheart, it's obvious that he always has. Unfortunately he didn't know how to tell you." He grinned down at her. "Not all men have my sterling way with words."

Davina tried to return Sam's smile, but the effort fell decidedly flat as she was forced once again to consider a life without him. "I'm going to miss you." The lump in her throat constrained her voice to a hoarse whisper.

"Hey," he responded on a hearty note that was entirely feigned, "what makes you think I'm going anywhere?"

Her eyes flew open. "Are you saying—" Her words drifted off as she took a sudden interest in a vivid mural on the far wall. She didn't want Sam to view the blatant hope she knew must be showing in her eyes.

He ran his hands up her arms, the gesture meant to reassure. "After all we've been through together the past three weeks, if you think I'm not going to stick around and see how this thing ends, you're not nearly as intelligent a lady as we both know you to be."

Davina was stunned by the effect that simple declaration had on her. Although she knew that she could not permit

Sam to remain here in the city with her for an indefinite period of time, she found that his willingness to do so meant more to her than she ever could have suspected. She had not allowed herself even the faintest hope of commitment or permanency from this man. The fact that he was so freely offering them was almost more than she could bear.

Davina valiantly fought back the threatening tears, vowing not to cry. A sense of humor she thought she had lost hours ago rose to the surface to keep the moment from becoming too intense, too compromising. She knew eventually there were things that would need to be said, but this wasn't the time to venture into such dangerous conversational territory.

"I suppose you expect me to continue paying your daily fee?"

Sam lifted a challenging brow. "I believe that *was* the agreement."

"The agreement was that you'd guide me to Naj Taxim."

"Which I believe I've done," he pointed out.

She nodded. "It appears so. It also appears that having successfully concluded your mission, we no longer have a contract."

"So now the lady wants to renegotiate?" he murmured, narrowing his eyes.

Davina gave him a satisfied smile. "I told you once before, Mr. McGee, that we Yankees are very astute business people."

"So you did." He ruffled his fingers through her short blond curls. "I also seem to remember you alleging that a Yankee recognizes exceptional value when she sees it." He ran his hand over her shoulder, satisfied as he felt her slight tremor.

"That's true," she admitted in a soft voice. His hand was moving ever so slowly downward. "Damm it, Sam, you're cheating."

He brushed her nipple with the pad of his thumb. "Just good negotiating tactics, sweetheart," he averred with a wicked grin. "Besides, if you want to know the truth, I never intended to stick to that overpriced fee in the first place. I may be good, but even *I* am not that good."

"Then why—"

"I was trying to get you to hightail it back to the States. That was before I realized how hardheaded you were."

Davina laughed, as she was supposed to. She looked down at their joined hands. "You're not ever going back, are you, Sam?"

Sam let out a long breath. He owed it to her to be honest. "I don't know. I can't see myself living in either Philadelphia or New York anytime in the near future; I've gotten used to life down here."

Davina took the next step cautiously, feeling as if she were suddenly walking an emotional tightrope—without a net. "But your life in Calderitas," she said slowly, carefully, "isn't exactly real."

He considered that, his thumb absently stroking her palm. "It may not come with all the trappings," he admitted. "But it is real, Davina. At least it is to me."

His words brought an unexpected flood of anguish as Davina was forced to face the fact that within days—perhaps hours—their paths would separate. Sam would return to his cantina and fishing boat in Calderitas, and as much as she truly loved him, Davina could not envision herself living above that rustic cantina, forced to put up with the fistfights, the drunken sailors and all the other unpleasant realities of life in a tropical harbor town.

No, she admitted, she could no more live that way than Sam could return to the elegant splendor of high tea at the Bellevue-Stratford, or attending Sunday-afternoon performances of the acclaimed Philadelphia Orchestra.

She closed her eyes, hoping that if she accepted it now, when the time came to say goodbye, she would have become adjusted to the idea. But as she allowed the sorrow to flow through her, entering her blood to infiltrate every cell, Davina knew with a fatalism she had not been aware of possessing that she would carry this heartache with her for the rest of her life.

Watching her intently, Sam was not unaware of Davina's distress. He wished that there was something he could say—anything—that might offer some glimmer of optimism. But he could think of nothing, short of lying, that would comfort her. So he remained silent, having to content himself with impotently stroking her hair, wishing that they were any two different people.

"I'm sorry about your father," he said after they had sat there in the darkening shadows for a long, silent time happy to simply hold each other.

"It's ironic, isn't it?" she murmured into his chest. "For fifteen months I refused to believe the reports of his death. Despite all the advice to the contrary, I came all this way through that jungle in order to prove he was alive."

He brushed an errant curl off her forehead. "You were right."

Her turquoise eyes, as she lifted them to his, revealed the distress she was feeling in her soul. "I was right," she agreed flatly. "And wrong."

He pressed his lips against her temple, breathing in her warmth, her scent. "Hey, let's not overlook the little fact that you were also right about Naj Taxim. You really found it, Davina. The fabled lost city of the Maya."

"I found something even more important," she whispered. "I found you."

Simple words, but they had the effect of rocking Sam to the core. Staring down at the top of her head, he forced himself to evaluate his reaction. He was not particularly surprised that he had no control over the rush of emotion her soft declaration had brought; he had surrendered his life to her the moment Davina had walked in the door of the cantina—it had just taken him awhile to accept that fact.

What Sam was discovering to be an overwhelming idea was that he had no intention of letting her out of his life. If it meant staying here with her in Naj Taxim until Jordan's death, that's precisely what he would do. And then, somehow, they would manage to find some middle ground that would enable them to spend the rest of their lives together. Sam had no idea where that place might be, or how they might accomplish such an unlikely feat, but with a determination that he had not felt since his King Midas days on Wall Street, he vowed that he would not let Davina Lowell get away.

Outside the room there was a sudden shout, followed by an excited babble of voices. Going to the door, Davina looked out over the compound.

In the lambent moonlight, the pyramid being erected to the Sun Jaguar loomed pale and lovely and sad. But that sight only held Davina's attention for a moment as the earth under her feet began to groan and tremble—tremendous pressures seeking release.

All around them people were reacting in various ways. Some were praying, beseeching ancient gods to protect them from harm. Others were hurriedly gathering up their possessions—chickens, blankets, looms, cooking utensils—preparing for evacuation. Still others had run off into the jungle, headed toward the secret cave. Davina frantically searched the chaotic scene for her father.

"There he is," Sam said, pointing across the compound to where Jordan Lowell was crossing the square in the center of the city.

"We have to save him!" Davina cried out.

Sam didn't like the ominous rumbling of the earth under his feet. "Wait here. I'll go get him."

He had gone no more than three steps when he turned. "If anything happens, your first priority—your *only* priority—is to yourself. Stay in the open. And whatever you do, don't panic."

With that, he turned on his heel, heading toward the pyramid. A moment later, Davina was by his side. "Dammit, I told you to stay put," he complained gruffly.

"I couldn't do that."

He shook his head. "One of these days you and I are going to have a long, meaningful discussion concerning feminine acquiescence."

"I refuse to believe you'd be happy with a clinging vine of a woman."

Sam looked down at her challengingly. "So what makes you think I'm happy with the hardheaded, stubborn one I've got?"

"Aren't you?"

He squeezed her hand. "Unbelievably."

As they approached Jordan, his face appeared even more drawn and haggard than it had been earlier. "Davina, I've been speaking with the Sun Jaguar; he's promised to give you and Samuel safe conduct back to civilization."

Davina's jaw lifted. "I'm not going anywhere."

Jordan Lowell's famous composure disintegrated as he stared at Davina. "What are you talking about?"

"I'm staying here with you."

Jordan exchanged a long look with Sam. "I don't suppose you could change her mind?"

Sam shook his head. "Not a chance. Not that I'd try. She loves you, Jordan. And I love her. So, you just happen to be stuck with both of us."

Jordan's eyes misted. "I don't know what's the matter with me today," he complained. "I'm acting like an old woman."

Reaching out, he embraced Davina, burying his lips in her hair. "Just like your mother," he murmured brokenly.

He turned toward Sam. "You will take good care of her, won't you, Samuel?"

Feeling an unwelcome lump in his own throat, Sam swallowed before answering. "You know I will, Jordan."

The older man nodded. "Good."

His attention turned to the house, which was beginning to rock on its foundation. "The journals! I must save them!" he decided suddenly.

Davina grabbed his arm. "Daddy—"

"Jordan," Sam broke in on a harsh note of warning. "Unless I'm sorely mistaken, this entire place is about to blow."

"This is my life's work we're talking about," Jordan argued, shaking Davina's hand away. "Samuel, keep my daughter here; I'll be right back." He turned away and headed back toward the house.

The vibrations beneath the earth's surface were increasing—not by much, but the difference was easily perceptible. Having once experienced a small tremor in Mexico City, Davina now shared Sam's conviction that unseen forces of nature had strained the bedrock, triggering the shifting of the earth's plates. There was no way of predicting the intensity of the impending earthquake, but she knew that their present position, adjacent to this enormous pyramid of limestone, was unreasonably dangerous.

"Daddy, you have to come with us!" Davina called out. The ground began emitting low, growling sounds.

Before she could argue further, the low growls became jackhammer-level roars. It was impossible to tell if the catastrophic rumbling was coming from the earth or the sky; it filled their heads, growing louder and louder until Davina was certain her eardrums would surely burst. She was flung to the ground, where she clawed at the rocky soil in a desperate attempt to keep from slipping off the face of the earth.

Beside her, Sam was on his hands and knees, trying to reach her as the earth rolled sickeningly underneath them, like a tidal wave at full bore. Suddenly the tremor stopped and the earth was firm again. An ominous quiet surrounded them.

"Thank God," Davina whispered, reaching out toward Sam. "Oh, thank God."

Her fingers had barely brushed his when the earth came alive again, the forces harsher, wilder this time. Before her disbelieving eyes, a cleft ripped open between her and Sam. Fighting for balance, cursing over the deafening roar, Sam fought for a foothold as the fissure threatened to swallow him into a pit of mud and stone. Davina hurled herself toward the maw, managing to capture Sam's wrist just before he slid below the rim of the chasm.

She was lying on her stomach, legs stretched out behind her, and she was slowly, inexorably, being pulled into the pit with Sam. Over the roar in her ears she could hear him shouting at her to release her hold on him, but she refused to listen, concentrating instead on keeping the fingers of both her hands wrapped tightly around his bruised wrist.

Just when she thought she could hold on no longer, they were given a respite as the tremor blessedly ceased once again. Using his feet against the side of the abyss, Sam fought his way out of the pit. They rolled away from the edge, lying together, gasping for breath.

"You damn fool," Sam managed to grind out. "You could have been killed!"

"So could you," Davina pointed out. "Besides, I don't remember you standing idly by when I fell into the cenote."

Sam knew he should be grateful to Davina; the rational part of his mind realized that he should be thanking her for saving his life. But fear for her own safety had fueled his fury and all he could think of was that she had taken a foolish risk.

"Dammit, that's different! If there's one thing you're going to have to accept, Davina, it's—"

At that moment there was another shock, stronger even than the previous two. The thunder surrounding them was punctuated by the screaming of birds, the screeching of stone against stone as the buildings of Naj Taxim began to split apart, flinging stone and rubble through the air. Looking around, Davina cried out in a sound that could not be heard over the roar of the earth's destruction. But Sam saw the terror in her eyes and turned his head in the direction she was staring.

Half walking, half crawling, Jordan was making his way back to the house. He had reached the base of the Sun Jaguar tomb when suddenly the mortar and stone began to crumble down, covering him in its wake. Davina screamed as she watched her father being buried alive.

Then everything fell silent.

"Wait," Sam cautioned, reaching out to restrain Davina from attempting to near the pile of rubble.

But he need not have bothered. She was staring at the spot where she had last seen her father.

Her rainbow-hued cotton dress was torn and filthy, her face streaked with dirt and mud. Sometime during the earthquake she had put her teeth through her lower lip; it was bleeding, but she didn't appear to notice.

Sam pressed his forehead against hers, closing his eyes against the wave of emotion stronger than anything nature had managed to conjure up in the past several minutes. Relief, despair and something stronger that he now knew was love.

"I thought I'd lost you," he murmured into her hair.

Davina was still numb; her eyes were huge emotionless wells as she looked around the city. Here and there a chicken that had escaped the debacle staggered over the rocks. They could hear a goat bleating plaintively, and the birds were still screaming their raucous fear to the heavens.

"Gone," she said flatly. "It's all gone. Naj Taxim, my father, everything. All gone."

Disturbed by her tone, Sam left her for a moment, returning to the house, which had miraculously escaped destruction. When he returned, he was carrying Jordan's journals.

"Not all gone," Sam insisted. He captured her chin in his fingers and directed her gaze to the books he placed in her lap. "It's all here, Davina. The city, the legend, your father. You can give them life again. It's what Jordan wanted."

Tears flooded her eyes and poured down her cheeks as she began crying violently, passionately. Unable to do anything but hold her, Sam gathered her into his arms, murmuring words of consolation he had no way of knowing she heard.

There was nothing gentle about her weeping as she clung to him, nor was there anything restrained about the anguished sobs being wrenched from somewhere deep inside her.

"That's it, love," Sam encouraged, his arms strong around her. "This little cry is long overdue, let it all out."

Wrapping her arms around his waist, pressing her face against his bruised and battered chest, Davina did just that.

After the sobs had run their course and her tears had ceased to flow, she remained cradled in his arms, too exhausted to speak or to move. Her eyes stung, her throat was sore, her head throbbed. Despite her knowledge that there would undoubtedly be aftershocks, Davina had no desire to move from this spot.

"Feeling better?" Sam asked after a long, silent time.

She nodded faintly.

"Do you feel up to a long-overdue declaration of intentions?" he asked with a great deal more calm than he was feeling.

Davina heard the strain in Sam's voice and lifted her red-rimmed eyes to him. "You don't have to do this," she whispered. "I don't need the words, Sam."

He managed a self-deprecating smile. "I think I do."

He motioned toward the journals that lay scattered about them. "I'm truly sorry about your father, Davina. I know how deeply you cared for him. I realize that he'll always be your first love."

"Sam—" She lifted a hand in a faint gesture.

"No." He covered her mouth with his, the kiss short and intense. "I'll admit to being a bit jealous of your feelings for Jordan in the beginning. It was obvious that you adored him."

Seeing the pain return to her face, Sam rushed to finish his statement. "But I've come to terms with that; I no longer have any problems with your father being your first love, Davina. As long as you'll let me be your last."

Davina's eyes misted again, but this time her tears were born from love, not grief. She framed his face with her palms and as her soft turquoise eyes met his strangely wary gaze, Sam read the answer to his question.

"My last, and for always," she whispered, pledging her love with a kiss.

Epilogue

"WE'VE GOT a slight problem."

"Tell me something I don't know," Sam said, lifting his gaze from the pile of paperwork spread over the ancient rolltop desk to Davina, standing in the doorway of his office. "What is it this time? Plumbing? Or are we blowing fuses again?"

"The electrician assured me that we're all wired to code," Davina said reassuringly. "And as for the plumbing, Luis has arranged for his cousin to take a look at it next week."

Sam arched a dark brow. "I thought the electrician was his cousin."

"Different cousin," Davina explained with a grin. "Luis appears to have a very large family. We'll probably never run out of repairmen."

"At the rate we're going, we'll run out of money to pay them, though," he grumbled, riffling through the papers.

She crossed the room and perched on the corner of his desk. "Not with you running the show, we won't." She massaged the back of his neck. "You, my darling, are a financial wizard. Every room is booked through the end of the holiday season."

"Which means we're working Christmas."

She laughed. "My, my, whose idea was it to buy this rather rustic resort on one of the less populated islands?"

Her gaze drifted out the wide picture window, drinking in the sight of the jeweled surf caressing the snow-white sand of Islas Mujeres, off the Yucatán coast. The crescent-shaped bay, with its palm-fringed beach, was one of the most beautiful spots on earth; fortunately, the lack of available nightlife kept the island from being overrun by the tourist crowd who frequented Cancún. The guests who sought out Sam and Davina's lodge and adjacent guest cabins were seeking peace and quiet, an idyllic respite from the harried pace of the outside world.

"Mine," Sam admitted. "But five years ago it seemed like a good investment. After all, I didn't know how long my period of self-exile was going to last; as crazy I admittedly was in those days, I wasn't fool enough to leave myself a pauper."

He scowled down at the bill in his hand. "Although Luis's relatives appear to be working toward that end."

Davina knew that Sam's decision to take an active interest in the running of the resort was his way of finding a compromise way for them to live. For her, though, it had never been a compromise; she had loved the island from the first moment she had seen it.

Not wanting a repeat of the Amazon tragedy, she had, as her father had suggested, taken the journals to the Mexican government. Together they had conceived a plan so she could describe the group of Maya without revealing their whereabouts. The remote location, accessible only through the secret cave, would help the city, which people were working to rebuild, remain hidden.

In the event that Naj Taxim was eventually discovered, the government had set up a contingency plan to instantly declare the entire area a sanctuary, permitting access only to a few chosen anthropologists. Once she'd finished her book, Davina planned to spend the next few years exploring the wealth of ruins the Yucatán had to offer.

"And who assured me that this would be the perfect retreat for me to work on my book about Naj Taxim?" she asked laughingly.

"Me, again."

"And who loves nothing better than taking the guests out on that smelly old boat everyday?"

"It's not that smelly," he protested.

"Darling," Davina countered patiently, "all fishing boats have a rather distinct odor. Yours included."

"You've never complained before," he grumbled.

"That's because you've kept the kitchen well stocked with fish; the guests love it."

She crossed her legs, displaying a glimpse of smooth, tanned thigh. It had been six months, and the sight of her never ceased to thrill him.

"Don't you want to know about our little dilemma?" she asked.

He ran his palm up her leg, reaching under the lightweight gauze dress. "I can think of other things I'd rather do."

She slapped his hand. "Not now. We have important matters to discuss."

Sam's fingers teased coaxingly at the hem of her dress. "What's more important than making love to my wife?"

"Family matters."

"Family matters? Are you all right? Is anything wrong?"

His smile instantly faded, concern darkening his amber eyes as he moved his gaze to her still-flat stomach. He wondered if he'd ever get used to the idea that she was carrying his child. Their child.

Davina pressed her palm against his face. "Nothing's wrong," she hastened to assure him. "It's just that I did something that I'm afraid you might not approve of."

"It wouldn't be the first time," he mumbled, thinking back on all the times Davina had shown herself to be a very headstrong female. But in all honesty, he had to admit that he wouldn't want her to be any other way.

"I wrote to your family, telling them about the baby."

Sam wasn't surprised. Luis's second cousin on his mother's side was the island's postmistress. Emilia had told him about the letter more than a week ago. Sam had been waiting for Davina to work up nerve to drop her little bombshell.

"And?"

She eyed him warily, suspicious of his easygoing attitude. Having expected fireworks at her act of subterfuge, Davina was worried that Sam's accepting behavior was merely the calm before a very violent storm.

"Your grandmother insists that when the baby is born we bring her great-grandchild to Philadelphia for the christening," she blurted out in a nervous rush of words.

Sam took his time to answer, arranging a stack of envelopes on the corner of his desk with careful precision.

Davina's nerves were literally screaming. "Sam?"

"I can't see any problem with that," he said finally.

She stared, waiting for the other shoe to fall. When it didn't, she flung her arms around his neck. "Just for a visit," she promised. "Then we'll come back home."

Home. Had ever a word sounded so wonderful? Sam wondered as he drew Davina onto his lap and covered her smiling lips with his own.

"Home," he agreed.

"You do like it here, don't you, Sam?" she asked, suddenly needing reassurance that he hadn't altered his life solely for her. "This *is* your favorite place in all the world, isn't it?"

"Not really."

"What?" She stared at him in utter disbelief.

In response, he rose abruptly to his feet, holding her effortlessly in his arms. "Come with me, sweetheart, and I'll show you my favorite place in all the world."

Guessing his intention, Davina laughed delightedly as Sam carried her out of the office and down the hallway to the cheery, sun-filled bedroom.

Harlequin Temptation

COMING NEXT MONTH

Can you keep a secret?

You can keep this one plus 4 free novels

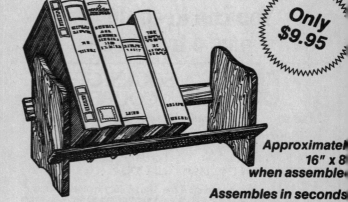